FEAST OF LIGHTS

To Jackie & family
with love & warm wishes

Ellen

Oct. 2/06

Feast of Lights

A YOUNG ADULT NOVEL BY

ELLEN S. JAFFE

SUMACH
PRESS

LIBRARY AND ARCHIVES CANADA CATALOGUING IN PUBLICATION

Jaffe, Ellen S.
Feast of lights : a young adult novel / Ellen S. Jaffe.

ISBN-13: 978-1-894549-60-8
ISBN-10: 1-894549-60-0

1. Hanukkah—Juvenile fiction. 2. Toronto (Ont.)—Juvenile fiction.
I. Title.

PS8619.A35F42 2006   jC813'.6   C2006-904344-2

Excerpt from *Fugitive Pieces* by Anne Michaels
used with permission from McLelland & Stewart Ltd.

Edited by Catherine Marjoribanks and Jennifer Day
Designed by Liz Martin
Cover photo (thanks to Greta Epstein) by Liz Martin

*Sumach Press acknowledges the support of the Canada Council
for the Arts and the Ontario Arts Council for our publishing program.
We acknowledge the financial support of the Government of Canada through
the Book Publishing Industry Development Program (BPIDP)
for our publishing activities.*

ONTARIO ARTS COUNCIL
CONSEIL DES ARTS DE L'ONTARIO

Printed and bound in Canada

Published by

SUMACH PRESS
1415 Bathurst Street #202
Toronto ON Canada M5R 3H8

sumachpress@on.aibn.com
www.sumachpress.com

Like other ghosts, she whispers;
not for me to join her, but so that,
when I'm close enough, she can push me
back into the world.

ANNE MICHAELS,
Fugitive Pieces

Dedication

To the memory of my great-grandmother, Mary Becker Axelrod (1872-1961), who travelled from Russia to New York City at age fourteen to join her parents and brothers, and who became the "Bubie" of our New York family,

to Rabbi Bernard Baskin and the memory of the late Marjorie Baskin (1927-2005), who taught me about Judaism and about humanity, compassion, integrity and courage,

and to Elizabeth Gilbert and Roger V. Gilbert and their extended families, whose loving generosity, goodness of heart and sense of humour have also helped me understand the meaning of family.

First Day:

"Look how it shines! Can we light the candles now?" Sarah's eyes were shining too in excitement. She felt like a little kid again, not a cool twelve-year-old. But tonight, that was okay.

"Of course. Why don't you light them yourself? You've done such a great job of cleaning Great-Grandma's menorah," her mother replied. "It looks beautiful, the way I remember it when I was your age."

The star and lions on the brass candle-holder glowed brightly, even before Sarah lit the candles. It was true, she *had* done a good job.

"That old thing!" she'd said when her mother first showed her the menorah a week ago. Her great-grandmother Ruth, now over ninety and living in a nursing home, had decided to give Sarah's family the heirloom her family had brought with them to Canada long ago. Ruth had kept it with her all these years until now, when she insisted that Sarah and her family use the old menorah to light the candles for the holiday of Hanukkah. She said it would bring them good luck. At least, that's how her mother explained it.

"She used the Yiddish word *glik*," Sarah's mother had said. "She had a hard time explaining the word in English, but finally she remembered it means 'luck and joy.' I guess we could use some of that." She took a deep breath. "She's speaking more Yiddish these days, the language her family spoke when she was growing up. I hardly remember any of the Yiddish words I used to know, but I could tell she really wanted us to have this menorah. Anyway, the residents aren't allowed to use candles in the home. I guess the staff is worried they'll set something on fire."

No wonder, Sarah thought. They're old. They forget things, and drop things, and you can hardly talk to them. Sarah didn't like to go to the nursing home. Her great-grandmother held her hand too tightly, and she smelled old and musty, like clothes packed too long in a trunk. Although she wasn't exactly forgetful or muddled, Sarah couldn't understand everything she said because she used a mixture of English and Yiddish. A mix of Hebrew with German and Eastern European languages, Yiddish was the old language that many Jews spoke in Europe and brought over to Canada and the United States, along with the few belongings in their suitcases. She'd once heard Ruth say that Yiddish was the language of the heart, but Sarah was sure her heart didn't speak that language. Not in Toronto in the twenty-first century.

Sarah's mother had put away the plain, silvery menorah the family usually used, and set the old brass menorah on the kitchen table. "I'll clean this up and it will be good as new," she'd said, but it sat there untouched for several days, gathering dust. Sarah, home alone and bored one day after school, decided to do her mother a favour and clean it herself. She scrubbed bits of hard, coloured candle wax out of the crevices with a toothpick and an old toothbrush dipped in hot water, and polished the metal with the cleanser that her mother kept under the kitchen sink.

Now she surveyed her work with pride, scraping off a trace of leftover wax with her fingernail. Tonight the menorah seemed to glow even more warmly and intensely — but maybe that was just the reflection of the bright lamps in the living room. As she looked at it, Sarah wondered how old the menorah was and where it had travelled over the years. She tried to imagine Great-Grandma Ruth polishing it when she was a girl. "Tell me again where your grandmother came from," she asked her mother.

"Well, she was born in Canada, here in Toronto. She was the youngest child. Her parents and older sisters came here by ship from the countryside in western Russia. Maybe it was part of what's now Poland," she added. "The borders got so mixed up with wars and treaties, I've never been quite sure where it was. My family never talked much about where they came from, anyway. When they did reminisce, it was about their own small *shtetl*, not the whole nation. And my grandmother said that once they arrived in Canada, they were so busy running their family grocery store, they didn't have time to talk about the past, so she didn't know much herself. Besides, they didn't want to remember the hard times. All Ruth knew was that they had been really poor and terrified by the pogroms, when soldiers on horseback galloped into their villages, burning houses and killing people for no reason. No wonder so many people emigrated."

"Like *Fiddler on the Roof* — in real life," Sarah said. She and her family had seen the musical a few years ago, performed by a local community theatre, and they had watched the movie too. She wondered what it would be like to live such a different life. She would miss a lot from her own time — but of course, if she'd lived back then, she wouldn't have known what she was missing.

"I guess so," said her mother, breaking into her thoughts. She handed Sarah the box of candles. "Here, you choose the colours."

Sarah picked a blue candle for the first night, and a white one to be the *Shamas*, the helper candle that lit all the others and had a special place on the menorah, higher than the rest. Sarah had bought the candles herself this year, making a detour to the market on her way home from school. She'd noticed that her mother hadn't got any, and she didn't want to have done all that cleaning for nothing. Besides, she looked forward to lighting them.

"Why can't you just use birthday candles?" her friend Marnie had asked her once. Marnie wasn't Jewish, and she was curious about their customs. Sometimes she asked questions that Sarah couldn't answer, but this one was easy.

"Because these are special," Sarah had told her. The candles were larger than birthday ones, a little thicker than a pencil and about as long as a stick of cinnamon.

"Isn't Dad going to light the candles with us?" she asked

now.

"I think he has to go out to a meeting. He said to just go ahead without him," her mother said, looking around the living room as if he might have come in while they were talking.

"We could wait," Sarah suggested. It wouldn't be the same without her father.

But her mother said, "Go on, it's okay."

Sarah remembered last year ... her father helping Ben to light the candles, Ben wanting to blow them out and make a wish, like he did for the candles on his birthday cake in October.

Sarah sighed and concentrated on striking the match, and it caught after two tries. She lit the *Shamas*, and then used the white candle to light the blue one. "*Baruch atoi Adonai ...*" she began, and her mother joined her. They continued, "... *Eloheinu melech ha'olam asher kideshanu bemitz-votav vetzivanu lehadlik ner shel Hanukkah.*"

They repeated the words in English:

"Blessed are you, Adonai our God, Ruler of the Universe, who makes us holy by your commandments, and tells us to kindle the Hanukkah lights."

The flame of the white candle quivered as she set it carefully back in place. Next to the blue one in its holder, seven small empty circles gaped like the open mouths of baby birds, each waiting its turn for a candle. They would add one more each night until there were eight candles, all burning together.

The two gleaming lions on the menorah looked as though they were guarding the flames. Above the lions was an ornate crown, topped by a six-pointed star. How beautiful it is, Sarah thought.

"Happy Hanukkah, darling," said her mother, giving Sarah a hug. Suddenly, they heard footsteps in the hallway and the sound of the front door opening. A gust of cold air blew into the room.

"I'm going out now," Sarah's father called. "See you later." The door slammed sharply behind him.

"Dad! Wait!" she cried.

"No, Sarah, let him go," said her mother, putting her hand, soft as a damp cloth, on Sarah's outstretched arm. "The holiday is hard for him this year."

Sarah turned away. What about me? she said to herself. It's hard for me, too. And for Mom. Sarah heard her mother rattling pots in the kitchen and realized she was alone in the room.

She sank down on the couch to watch the candles. It was a tradition — more like a rule — that you shouldn't do any work, not even homework, during the half-hour or so it took for the Hanukkah candles to burn down. Her mother had told her that, in the past, people often put menorahs in the window to light up the dark night. You were supposed to light the candles at sunset but today had been so grey and cloudy, the sun hadn't come out at all.

She was glad it was Friday. School was over for the week, plus Friday evening was also the beginning of the Jewish Sabbath. Sarah and her family used to have a special dinner on most Friday nights, to welcome the weekly holiday. They would light two candles and have braided *challah* bread, light and delicious. Sometimes they'd go to her grandparents' house; on other nights her grandparents would come to theirs. But they hadn't had Friday night dinners for a long time. Sarah didn't miss them so much, but she really cared about Hanukkah. She couldn't believe her father didn't want to celebrate the holiday this year. It would be a very long eight days!

Tomorrow she'd dig out her old picture book of Jewish holidays and look over the Hanukkah story. She always forgot some of the details. Where had she last seen that book? She'd hunt for it in the morning; tonight she was just too tired. Her head drooped as she watched the candles. The room felt cold, and Sarah got up to check if the front door was closed tight — yes, it was. She trudged back to the couch and lay down with her head resting on a cushion and her feet, in their old red-striped socks, propped up on the far end of the couch.

The last time she had worn these socks she had been rocking in the hammock at Marnie's cottage, listening to the waves of the lake lapping against the shore. The memory made her feel peaceful and warm. She watched the candle flames flicker as if caught in a sudden wind, then sparkle brightly. She closed her eyes, and her left leg jerked suddenly, the way it sometimes did just before she fell asleep.

As she lay there, Sarah felt the rocking become even stronger, as if the couch had become the hammock. No — not a hammock; it was more like being rocked by waves in a rowboat or a canoe. She could hear water sloshing nearby, and a ship's foghorn. A ship? What was going on? She began to feel queasy, as if she were seasick, and she realized she was actually inside a ship. It wasn't a puny rowboat or canoe, but something bigger, much bigger. She was lying on a scratchy wool blanket that smelled dirty, like old food, even a bit like someone had peed on it. There were other odours — salty sea air, smoke, sweaty bodies. She could hear people talking in low voices and moving restlessly. A baby cried and the noise grated on her ears. She opened her eyes but at first she could hardly see anything in the gloomy darkness. Then, as she became used to the dim light, she saw that she was in a huge room full of people, mainly women and children. She could hear water slapping and engines throbbing noisily, but when she looked up she saw only a metal ceiling. She wished she were up on deck where she could see the water and the sky.

Just then, out of the blue, came the sound of music playing — fast, light notes almost like laughter. She could hardly believe her ears. Where was it coming from? She sat up with a jolt, looked around and saw a tall man with a fierce red beard. There was a flash of silver at his mouth and she saw that he was playing a small metal harmonica, almost hidden in his huge hand. He seemed to glide among the people, dancing to his own music. A group of children gathered around him and started singing along. Sarah edged closer to them — the lively music made her happy, even though she couldn't understand the words. She settled herself next to a girl about her own age who had long red hair, just a shade darker than the man's. The girl smiled at Sarah and didn't seem surprised to see her sitting so close. Maybe with so many people here, no one worried about being jostled by strangers.

Sarah admired the girl's hair, which was a deep chestnut colour and fell like a curtain over the baby she rocked in her arms. Sarah had dark brown hair, like both her parents, but her mother had told her that red hair ran in her family and Sarah had always wished she'd inherited that.

As he played, the tall man bent down and tousled the hair of the red-headed girl, then gently touched the baby's cheek. The girl smiled up at him and Sarah guessed that he was their father. After a while, the tempo of the music slowed down and became soft and dreamy, reminding Sarah of feather beds and lullabies. Then the man slipped his harmonica into the pocket of his worn overcoat and began singing in a deep, comforting voice.

Rozhinkes mit mandlen
Dos vet zayn dayn baruf
Yidele vets alts handlen
Shlof zhe, Yidele, shlof.

At first she didn't have a clue what the Yiddish words meant, but then, amazed, she found that suddenly she could understand them, the way she sometimes knew things in dreams.

Raisins and almonds, everything sweet
You will grow rich living in the new land
All good things will come into your hands
So sleep, my little one, sleep.

As he sang, babies, children and even some of the women began to fall asleep. Their snoring sounded like loud purring. Sarah felt as if she could go on listening forever, and she noticed that her seasickness had almost disappeared. She wished she had some raisins and almonds to eat, right then and there.

A child started to cry, breaking into her reverie.

"Wolf! Wolf!" she heard someone calling, a woman's voice rising over the child's wailing.

Looking around, she saw a wide-eyed woman in a blue kerchief grasp the arm of the bearded musician. A little girl, crying loudly, clung to her skirt. Dazed, Sarah thought of the phrase "Cry Wolf," but then she figured out that Wolf must be the man's name. A strange name in a strange place. He whispered something to the woman, then crouched down to kiss the little girl's cheek. Smiling, he picked up the child, swung her high in the air and set her down gently as her crying stopped. The woman leaned down to the red-haired girl next to Sarah, gave her a hug and kissed the sleeping baby. *"Zisseh-maydela,"* she whispered softly to the girl. Sweet girl, thought Sarah, delighted she had recognized the words. Sarah breathed in — the woman smelled like fresh-baked *challah*. With a deep sigh, the mother hoisted the little girl onto her hip and carried her through the crush of people toward some wooden benches attached to the wall. With a fold of her skirt, she dusted off a place to sit and eased herself down, letting the little girl stretch out next to her. Sarah watched the child wriggle a bit, then rest her head in the woman's lap.

The ship lurched suddenly, and as Sarah tried to steady herself, she grasped the red-haired girl's arm for a moment. "Sorry," she said, but the girl didn't seem upset and even wrapped her right arm around Sarah's shoulder, cradling the sleeping baby with her left. The tall man, Wolf, reached out and put his big hand, covered with red-gold hairs, on the other girl's head for a moment, then he patted Sarah's head, too. "*Meyn kinder*," he said. "Happy Hanukkah, *meyn kinder*." "My children," he was saying. She wondered why the man included her in his greeting. Was it just because she was there?

"We have no candles to light here on this ship," the man said, "but it is still a holiday. I hope we will find a sweet life, like a miracle, in the new land." Even though she didn't know him, Sarah found his voice comforting.

The girl beside her started to nod off, her head resting on Sarah's shoulder. She muttered in her sleep as though she were dreaming. The baby dozed in her lap, snuffling noisily. Sarah thought she heard someone call her name, but to her surprise, it was the man Wolf speaking to the girl next to her. "*Sha*, Sarah, *sha, sha*," he said. Was this girl also named Sarah? That was possible — it wasn't such an unusual name. "My Sarah, my little Saraleh," he added, kissing her forehead.

Wolf made sure that the girl was sleeping peacefully then made his way over to the benches to join the woman and the little girl. Watching them, Sarah decided that the woman must be his wife, and the other Sarah, the younger girl and the baby were all their children. "Saraleh," she repeated to herself — the nickname had a nice sound. She was trying hard to make sense of everything that was happening around her, but then Wolf began playing his harmonica softly and her thoughts drifted with the melody.

Abruptly, the ship's foghorn gave a sharp, mournful cry and Sarah felt a wave of homesickness. She missed her clean, comfortable, modern house. This place smelled of sweat, urine, cooked cabbage and other things she couldn't name. The people's faces looked pinched and scared, as if fear were something they could taste. Was this how her great-great-grandparents had felt on their long journey to Canada all those years ago? She tried to imagine leaving home and setting off for a strange country, not even knowing the language and only able to pack a few necessary items: a change of clothes, blankets and a couple of treasures — perhaps a menorah or a harmonica.

The air felt close and sticky and was making her feel sick again — she really needed some fresh air. She felt a breeze and, turning toward it, she saw a metal stairway that she hadn't noticed before. It seemed to lead to the upper deck. Through the opening at the top of the stairs she could see people standing against a rope railing, and smokestacks jutting up into the cloudy sky.

She stood up carefully so she wouldn't disturb the girl

next to her. Pushing through some damp shirts and sheets hanging on a makeshift clothesline, she reached the narrow stairs and climbed up, holding tight to the banister and counting each step — seven in all — as the ship rolled and lurched. When she reached the top, she picked her way toward a clear space by the side of the ship, ducking around groups of people huddled in old coats, shawls, even blankets.

When Sarah looked over the guardrail into the murky, grey-green water, she drew in her breath sharply. It was so deep, and the waves crashed violently as far as she could see. She shivered in the sudden cold, and icy spray swirled upward, stinging her face, smelling of salt and sea creatures. The sensation made her skin crawl — but she couldn't stop looking downward, mesmerized by the rushing waves. She felt herself pulled down, down, deeper down …

"Watch you don't fall," said an old woman next to her, grasping her arm firmly with gnarled fingers.

A teenage boy wearing a green muffler chimed in, "Look at her with those fancy clothes! But don't put on airs and go over to first class." He winked, and she realized he was just trying to be friendly.

Even surrounded by all these people, Sarah felt alone. She was scared, but there was also something thrilling about being on her own in the middle of the ocean, not knowing how she'd gotten here. Another blast of the foghorn, loud as a siren, made her jump backward, almost losing her balance. As she grabbed hold of the rail again, she noticed more mist and fog swirling around her, thicker and thicker.

The next thing she knew, Sarah felt a rush of clean warm air. She opened her eyes and found herself back in her own living room, sitting on the couch in front of the menorah. Both candles had burned down, and two thin plumes of smoke rose in the air. Her body felt stiff and chilly-damp, as if she had been out in the rain.

Dazed, she looked at her watch. Only forty minutes had passed since the candles were lit, but she felt as though she had been on that ship for hours. Could she have fallen asleep and had some kind of weird dream? Yes, that made sense. It must have been brought on by her mother's mention of their family's journey to Canada.

She stood up, rubbing her hands to warm them, and headed into the kitchen. Her mother had left a plate of sandwiches and a glass of milk on the table, with a note saying that she was tired and going to bed early. Still puzzling over her experience, Sarah ate her supper without really tasting it and climbed the stairs to her room. She didn't feel like watching TV or even turning on the computer. She got into bed and read for a while but couldn't concentrate because the dances and lullabies of Wolf's harmonica were playing over and over in her mind. The music kept on even when she turned off the light. Where had these songs come from? She was sure she'd never heard them before.

The people she'd met on the ship had seemed so real. But by the look of their clothing and the age of the ship, they must have been from a long time ago. She shook her head.

It would be impossible to go back in time like that — such things only happened in stories or movies. She must have fallen asleep on the couch and had one of those very vivid dreams that feel like they're really happening. Or perhaps it was a daydream, the kind of story she sometimes made up to help her get to sleep. She felt exhausted, as if she'd actually been on the crowded old ship. Thinking about it made her even more tired, but she struggled to stay awake to figure it all out. She heard the sound of her father opening the front door, and wondered if she should tell him about what had happened. But before she knew it, she fell asleep.

Second Day:

SATURDAY, DECEMBER 7

Whoosh, swhoosh. Wind blowing against the trees outside her window woke Sarah early the next morning. As she lay curled up in her cozy blanket, she felt as if she were back on the ship, rocking gently with the waves. She kept her eyes closed, enjoying the sensation. She could still feel Wolf's soothing hand on her hair and hear the sound of his music. There had been a lullaby about raisins and almonds but she couldn't recall all the words. As she remembered the people she'd seen, she realized the sleeping baby reminded her of Ben when he was a baby. She hadn't thought about that last night, but there had been something familiar in the shape of his head, the way his lips moved when he slept. But maybe all babies looked like that.

Once more, she puzzled over what had happened when she had lit the Hanukkah candles. The most logical explanation was that meeting Wolf and Saraleh had been the kind of magical dream that you wish you could keep on dreaming. And yet — she could feel a tug at her heart, an unshakeable feeling that she had really been there and met all those people.

Only when the familiar, golden-crisp aroma of her mother's *latkes* tickled her nose did she know for sure that she was in her own bed, in her own house — and she was glad! Her mother always made the delicious potato pancakes for Saturday brunch during Hanukkah. She'd better hurry if she was going to help!

Sarah dressed quickly in her favourite old jeans and red sweater, and flew down the stairs. Her mother was busy making the *latkes*. You had to grate raw potatoes and mix them with eggs, onion and a little lemon juice and flour, then fry them. It was traditional to eat them during this holiday because they were cooked in oil, and oil was an important part of the Hanukkah story. She remembered last year when she'd told the story to Ben. A long time ago, the Jewish people had to clean and fix up their holy temple, but they found only enough holy oil for one day, and it would take over a week to get more. By a miracle, their little vial of oil lasted for eight days, and ever since then, people had celebrated Hanukkah by lighting candles for eight nights and cooking special foods with oil. Now, of course, people used electricity and often worried about eating fried foods, but Sarah always looked forward to the once-a-year treat of *latkes*.

"What can I do?" she asked, hurrying into the kitchen.

"Nothing, sweetie, everything's just about finished."

"But Mom, you said this year I could help make the *latkes*. You said it last year. You *promised.*"

"I'm sorry, Sarah, I must have forgotten," her mother said. She sounded tired, even though she'd gone to bed early.

Sarah kicked at a chair while her mother's back was turned. She and Mom never seemed to do things together anymore. It was even worse now than when Ben was so sick. At least then she'd been able to do things to help out. She sighed. She had really wanted to learn to make *latkes*.

But she couldn't stay mad too long; the pancakes smelled too good.

Her father came in to the kitchen and ruffled her hair. "How's my favourite daughter?" he asked. It was an old joke. Ben used to protest, "What about me?" and Dad would answer, "I didn't say, 'My favourite son,' did I?"

Now the words fell flat, flatter than the pancakes.

Her father sat down at the table and started doing the crossword puzzle in the newspaper.

"What's an eight-letter word for snowstorm?" he asked.

"Blizzard," Sarah answered right away, pleased with herself.

"Mmm. I guess so. Thanks." But he didn't look up, and for some reason he sounded mad. Cross words indeed, Sarah thought. He seemed to brighten up, however, when the food was ready.

"*Latkes,* eh?" he said. "Smells good. And just right for the holidays." Her mother quietly put three steaming pancakes on each plate, and they all sat down at the table.

They spooned sour cream and applesauce onto the *latkes*. Some of Sarah's friends thought that sounded yucky, but they changed their minds fast enough when they tried them. So many people from all over the world lived in their neighbourhood that the kids were used to tasting different foods at each other's houses. It made life more interesting. Sarah loved the *callaloo* that Marnie's mother served. Half soup, half stew, it tasted awesome; a spinach dish that was actually edible! Marnie's mother was from Trinidad, and Marnie and her family often went back to visit. Lots of her cousins came up to Toronto, too — usually in the summertime.

The *latkes* were so delicious, and Sarah was so absorbed in her own thoughts, that she didn't notice the tension growing in the room, thick as sour cream. But then the sharp edge in her father's voice made her pay attention.

"Excellent *latkes*," he said, wiping his mouth. "But tell me, Rachel, are we going to go through every single holiday ritual?"

"Why not?" asked her mother.

"Not much point, this year."

"Hanukkah still means something to me — and to Sarah," she answered.

Sarah's eyes burned and she felt the *latkes* heavy in her stomach.

A little muscle stiffened in her father's neck. "Let Sarah speak for herself," he said in a low voice. "Are you in the holiday mood, sweetheart?"

Sarah shook her head, but he'd put the question all wrong. She wasn't feeling festive, but she still wanted the *latkes,* the *dreidel,* the menorah. She knew that somehow they would make her feel better. She looked down at her plate and mumbled, "Well, not exactly, but ..."

"Speak up!"

"Don't put her on the spot, Michael. You can celebrate without feeling ..." Her mother paused, searching for the right word. "Without forgetting."

"Life has to go on, eh?" her father said in a mocking tone. "Well, I can forget the holidays for this year — and probably forever!"

Sarah nearly choked on her mouthful, but she swallowed hard and blurted out, "No, Dad! I want the potato pancakes, and the candles and everything."

"You still have a daughter. She needs you, too," her mother said quietly.

It's all Ben's fault, Sarah thought fiercely. Why did he have to get leukemia? Why did he have to die? Why couldn't we just go on the way we were, when we were happy?

She didn't want to make her father even angrier, but she had to say something. "I do want to have Hanukkah, Dad," she said. Just as fiercely as she'd been mad at Ben, she now felt a rush of love for him. It was awful — no one would even mention his name. Did she dare?

"I think Ben would like us to do it," she began. "Remember how he always wanted to put maple syrup on the *latkes*, like ordinary pancakes?" There. She had said it. His name. Her parents were quiet; maybe it wouldn't be so bad after all.

Her father looked at her for a long moment before he spoke. "I'm sorry, Sarah," he said in his new voice, cold as a blizzard. "I thought you were more grown-up. Maybe you still want these things, but I just can't do it this year." He stood up and strode out of the room, not looking back.

Sarah couldn't stop the tears. Her mother patted her hand, then got up and gave her a hug, and Sarah hugged her back. Mom looked as if she was going to cry, too, but then she sat back down and said, "He'll be all right. Give it time."

Sarah made herself eat the remaining potato pancakes on her plate. She had to eat slowly, not gobble them down as usual, or she might throw up. Her mother was eating carefully, too, and stirred two extra spoonfuls of sugar into her coffee without even noticing. When they cleared the table, they left her father's plate sitting there with his half-finished food until, sure he wasn't coming back, her mother finally threw the leathery, cold *latkes* into the garbage.

Sarah went over to her best friend Marnie's for the afternoon. She'd been spending more time there over the last year or so. It had started when Ben first got sick, and her parents spent hours visiting him in the hospital, often staying overnight while he had his chemotherapy treatments. Sarah would go to Marnie's for dinner and to sleep over, then they'd walk to school in the morning.

When Ben came home and was still too sick to go to school for a while, Sarah always hurried home to play with him. If he was too tired for toys and games, she'd just sit with him, singing old songs, reading out loud or making up stories. They had a favourite one about "Three Little Plums" instead of three little pigs. Sometimes Marnie joined them, and sometimes Sarah went over to Marnie's when she needed a break.

Ben stopped going to school altogether after March break. The kids in his Grade 1 class sent him cards, and his teacher, Mrs. Bender, sometimes came to visit. He went back to the hospital for the last time a few weeks before school ended, and he died on July 1, Canada Day. What awful timing, when everyone else was celebrating, waving flags and setting off fireworks! She still couldn't look at the Canadian flag without tears coming to her eyes.

After Ben died, Sarah tried to help out at home, but her mother and father were so quiet the house felt like it was wrapped in fog. During *Shiveh,* the first week of mourning, relatives and friends kept coming and going, but after that nobody visited. The rest of the summer they didn't do much, didn't even go to the cottage as they usually did. At the end of August, Sarah's grandparents took her to Niagara Falls and they saw a play at the theatre in Niagara-on-the-Lake — a new version of *Peter Pan* — but she felt they were all too busy pretending they were cheerful to really have fun.

When school started again, Sarah started just going to Marnie's whenever things got tense at home. In Marnie's cheerful bedroom with yellow flowers on the wallpaper, they could listen to music, chat with their friends on MSN and gossip about boys at school, while at home Sarah felt she had to walk around on tiptoe. In mid-September came the Jewish New Year, Rosh Hashanah, but her parents didn't really put their hearts into the celebration. And Yom Kippur was just as bad — they didn't even observe the fast that day. But she did. She didn't even mind the fast this year, because food wasn't tasting good anyway. She felt like she needed to be forgiven for something, but she didn't know what she had done wrong. Surely things will be better soon, she had thought, but as autumn went on, nothing changed.

Still, Sarah had been convinced that life would improve by Hanukkah. Wasn't this a holiday celebrating miracles, when people were happy and light shone again?

She made sure to leave Marnie's before dark, to get home in time to light the candles. "How come Hanukkah comes on different days each year?" Marnie asked at the door. "Why can't it always be on the same day, like Christmas?"

"Well, it's not any old time — it always comes between the end of November and the end of December," Sarah said. "Around the winter solstice, I guess. It *does* always start on the same day in the Jewish calendar."

"Don't you get confused, with two different calendars?" asked Marnie.

"Well, we use the regular calendar for everyday things, like everyone else," Sarah said. "The Jewish calendar is mostly just for ceremonies and holidays. The months have different names, and there's another way of counting the days because each month starts with the new moon. It's hard to explain, but I know Hanukkah moves around between November and December because there's never an exact match between the calendars."

Marnie shook her head. "Sounds complicated."

"Well, it works," said Sarah. "Anyway, I've gotta get home now. I'll call you tomorrow."

She hurried back along the side streets to her house on Borden. There were only a few people outside, walking their dogs or coming home from shopping. Today had been sunny and now the sky glowed a deep orange, reminding her of the candles.

"Where's Dad?" she asked her mother as she hung up her jacket.

"Out with Uncle Mark," her mother told her. Uncle Mark was her father's older brother.

"I still want to light the candles, Mom," Sarah begged. "Especially with our new menorah."

Her mother hugged her. "Thank you for understanding my point of view."

Sarah pulled away. She didn't want to take sides — that wasn't what she'd meant. But she didn't say anything, just went over to the box of candles and began to prepare the menorah. As she set the candles in place, she thought about what had happened the night before. She'd been tired, fallen asleep and had a crazy dream. That was all. It couldn't happen again. She placed a blue candle on top, for the *Shamas*, and a red and a yellow one underneath: two on the second day. Tonight, her mother lit the *Shamas* and murmured the blessing while Sarah lit the other two candles. Then her mother went into the kitchen to make some tea. "I'll fix us some omelettes later," she promised.

Sarah watched the candles for a few minutes, then went to the bookcase and rummaged around until she found her *Golden Treasury of Jewish Holidays*. When she'd read the Hanukkah story to Ben last year, it had been hard for him to follow all the details. Maybe he would have liked it better this time.

The book began by saying that in the Jewish calendar, the holiday always began on the 25th day of the month named *Kislev*.

In 165 BCE, she read, the five Maccabee brothers and their followers fought against King Antiochus, who ruled the country of Judah and several other lands. Antiochus tried to force all the people in his kingdom, including the Jews, to believe in his own country's gods and customs. When the Jewish people refused to give up their own beliefs, Antiochus and his army took over the holy Temple in Jerusalem and threatened to kill anyone who didn't obey them.

But finally the Maccabees defeated Antiochus. When the people began to clean the Temple, they realized they had only enough holy oil for one day. They were supposed to keep a special light burning all the time in the Temple — it would go out if they ran out of oil, and it would take days to get more. What could they do?

Sarah had just reached this crucial part of the story when the room began to grow dark around her. The candle flames shone brighter and brighter, enveloping her in their glow. A faint musty smell filled the air, not like her living room at all. Not again, she thought. Her heart began to beat faster — first with fear, then anticipation. Yes — again! She had hoped this would happen. Maybe it wasn't only a dream. But if not, what was going on? She readied herself for another journey to the ship.

Sarah looked around as her eyes got used to the dim light. She certainly wasn't at home anymore, but she wasn't on the rolling ship, either. She was in a small building of some kind, seated on a hard wooden bench. Her head almost touched the ceiling, and she realized she was up in a balcony. All around her, on rows of benches, were women and girls, some holding babies. Most of the women were murmuring in low voices. Looking down to the floor below, she saw more benches where men and boys were sitting pressed close together.

The men were dressed in black, and wore the skullcaps called *yarmulkes* on their heads, and white shawls with long fringes draped over their shoulders. Facing them at the front of the room stood a rabbi with a full grey beard, but she couldn't make out what he was saying from up in the balcony.

Sarah leaned forward in curiosity as the rabbi turned around and opened the intricately carved doors of a large wooden cabinet. Inside was a thick scroll covered with a cloth, dark red and embroidered with a pattern of gold leaves.

Sarah's family went to synagogue only a few times a year, and their synagogue was very different from this one, but she recognized the scroll immediately. It was the *Torah,* the first five books of the Bible. And the wooden cabinet was called the Ark, just like the ship Noah built during the Flood. An oil lamp hung above the Ark, its flame sputtering. On the back wall were colourful paintings of musical instruments — a harp, a trumpet and something that resembled Wolf's harmonica — and of a deer and a lion, like pictures from an old storybook. The lion looked like the one on her menorah.

In Sarah's synagogue at home, men, women and children all sat together, so she was startled to see them separated here. This must be one of those traditional Orthodox synagogues, she thought, remembering her grandfather's stories about the old days. I really am going back in time, she thought. She looked more closely about her, searching for clues to where she might be.

Although it felt strange to be surrounded by women, Sarah liked the comforting smell of old dresses, flowers, flour and the spicy scent of cinnamon. No one paid her any attention, even though she was a stranger. As she watched and listened, the rabbi turned to face the room again. He began to speak directly to the people, his voice resonating as if he had switched on a microphone.

Like the people she had seen on the ship, he was speaking Yiddish. This time, she was not surprised that she could understand him clearly. "Today we say farewell to a family going to the New World," he said. Sarah peered down and saw the rabbi point at Wolf, the red-bearded man from the ship, standing downstairs with the men. Then, just ahead of her in the balcony, she recognized Saraleh, sitting with the woman in the blue kerchief, the younger girl and the baby. As the rabbi gestured toward them, Saraleh blushed almost as red as her hair.

Looking around, she noticed Sarah and gave her a quick, polite smile, the kind of smile you'd give a new kid in the class. She doesn't remember me, Sarah thought, even though we saw each other on that ship. But now they seemed to be even further back in time, before the voyage, so maybe that's why the girl didn't remember.

The rabbi continued, spreading his arms wide. "Today, at the beginning of Hanukkah, the Feast of Dedication and Light, we must not forget the miracles of the past that God showed to our people. Today we remember the miracle of the oil, which lasted for eight days. We tell our children and grandchildren the story of Mathias and his five sons, especially Judah Maccabee, the Hammer, the Lion of God, who rescued our people from the wicked King Antiochus when he tried to ruin our Temple with idols of stone."

As he spoke, Sarah imagined a huge temple, far bigger and shinier than this building, filled with statues of gods and goddesses in the form of animals and birds, like those she had seen at the Royal Ontario Museum. They had gone there on a school trip last year, when they were studying ancient cultures. She'd loved the ivory Inuit figures of whales and drummers, wooden raven masks from British Columbia, gleaming Egyptian statues of cats and crocodiles, colourful Chinese dragons. Were these "idols"? The museum guide had said these figures showed how different people saw the world and all the powerful forces in it.

"When the Maccabees finally drove out Antiochus' soldiers and priests from the Temple," continued the rabbi in his confident voice, "our people had the terrible and wonderful job of rebuilding and cleaning the Temple. Finally, all that remained to be done was to find holy oil for the Eternal Light — but this was the most important job of all. They searched and searched but found only a tiny vial of oil, barely enough for one day. It would take longer than that to make more or send for it from afar. The people had heavy hearts. What could they do? Only a miracle could save them."

The rabbi spoke so expressively Sarah could see herself in that ancient temple and hear the people wailing and crying. "Just wait," she wanted to shout out to them, "there *will* be a miracle! Everything will be all right."

Right at that moment, a baby started to cry. Sarah leaned forward to get a better look and saw it was the baby from "her" special family. "Shhh, my little one, *meyn kind, ah meyn kind*," Sarah heard the mother say, as she rocked the child in her arms. She watched Saraleh stroking the baby's hair to soothe him.

"Yes," the rabbi was saying, "there was a miracle. That little flask of oil burned steadily for eight days and eight nights. This is why we light candles for eight nights, lighting up our hearts and helping to lighten the darkness in the world. And why we repeat the words *Nes gadol haya sham,* — A great miracle happened there — and use them in the *dreidel* game our children play. They can see the letters as the tops spin round and round."

He paused, and people began murmuring restlessly. Sarah squirmed around on the hard bench, trying to find a more comfortable position.

"But that is not all, my friends," said the rabbi suddenly. "We will see miracles in our lifetime. Our beloved Wolf

Rifkin and his family will see miracles when they go to Canada. And we will all see miracles in our own lives, our own history. We are at the beginning of the twentieth century. May it bring hope for all of us."

Sarah felt the rabbi's gaze linger on her. He seemed to have X-ray vision — as if he could see right inside her and know that she didn't belong here. But of course he didn't know everything, certainly not about the future. Sarah knew that for Jews, life in Europe was going to get much harder. Wolf and his family were smart — and courageous — to leave. Just like her own ancestors had been.

But maybe, just maybe, the rabbi could tell her something about what was going on. How had she come here, to this place so long-ago and far away from her own home? And why?

The rabbi closed the doors of the Ark to end the service, and everyone was getting up to leave. Making her way down the narrow wooden stairs, Sarah found herself pressed against Saraleh, who was wearing a long-sleeved, navy blue dress and talking to a girl with shiny black hair and sad eyes. "Of course I'll miss you when we go to Canada, but who knows, Fagie, maybe soon you and your family will come over there, too. The rabbi said miracles could happen. And sometimes miracles are things you wish for." She tossed her red hair and lowered her voice conspiratorially. "You know what I think? I think God listens to women and girls just as much as to boys and men. After all, Mama says childbirth is a miracle, and only women can give birth."

"Shhh," said the other girl, putting a finger on her lips.

"Don't let Rabbi Elisha hear you talking like that. And it *would* take a miracle for me to come to Canada — I'd have to fly there like a bird!"

Sarah remembered how some of her mother's friends talked about God as "She" or "The Goddess," to honour women and girls. How would Saraleh feel about that?

"I'm going to a new world," the red-haired girl was saying to Fagie. "I'm sure things will be different there."

"Different? Just a little," Sarah chuckled to herself as she overheard their conversation. Saraleh turned and looked at her as they reached the bottom of the stairs.

"You must be new, I haven't seen you here in *shul* before. But you agree with me, don't you? You *can* wish for miracles." She touched Sarah's arm affectionately, then she and Fagie darted outside through the heavy, carved door.

Sarah didn't think she believed in miracles. Maybe they used to happen, or people believed they did, but not now. They're just a bunch of old stories. You can't prove them scientifically, she thought to herself. The technology she and her friends used every day might seem miraculous to people who had never seen computers, airplanes, television or even a telephone or a radio. But a real miracle, if it ever happened, would probably scare the pants off you. Even the rabbi wouldn't know what to do.

As she stood at the threshold, hesitating, the rabbi came up to her. He smelled old and dusty, a little like Great-Grandma Ruth, but not unpleasant. He smiled at her kindly.

"You, too, are looking for a miracle, is that not right?" he asked.

"I don't know," Sarah said. "I don't know if miracles ..."

"If they exist?" the rabbi asked. "More things exist in life than we can see with our eyes or hear with our ears," he went on. "You don't ... live here, do you?"

Sarah wasn't sure what the rabbi meant, but she wanted to answer him honestly. "No," she said, "I don't. And I don't know what I'm looking for."

"We don't find miracles when we go looking for them," he said softly. "But sometimes they find us. You are welcome in our midst today. Now go in peace, my child."

"Wait," Sarah said, before he could walk away.

"What is it? You have a question for me?"

"Yes. What happened after the miracle? After the oil lasted for eight days? What did they do next?"

The rabbi looked puzzled. "The story ends after eight days," he said. "The oil lasted so long — that was the miracle. What else is important?" He stroked his beard. "Now that you ask, I think that after the miracle they simply went on with their lives. They got more oil and finished cleaning the Temple, they prayed and worked, ate and slept, raised their children, and they did not have to fight again for many years. We do not tell that story because it is the tale of ordinary life, day after day after day."

"Isn't that important, too?" Sarah asked.

"Why are you asking me these things?" the rabbi said impatiently. "Ordinary life is the story of women and children and men who work with their hands, not the story of great heroes, scholars and leaders." He paused, and looked at her curiously. "But yes, after war and hardship, perhaps ordinary life is precious and valuable. Precious as oil and the salt that flavours our food. I will consider this." He turned and strode away.

Sarah's nose tickled with a mixture of smells — old clothing, garlic, musty books and people crowded together. She looked at the lamp burning over the Ark: not electric, like the one in her synagogue at home, but a real oil lamp. She watched, mesmerized, as the flame flickered like a distant star. She felt tired and didn't want to think about miracles, journeys or things being different. All this was giving her a headache. Dizzy and confused, she closed her eyes.

She opened her eyes to the glare of the electric lamps in the living room. The candles gave a final blaze and sputtered out. *You will see miracles*, said a voice inside her. It was calm and clear and Sarah wanted to believe it. She rubbed her eyes, and was surprised to find them wet with tears. Her head still ached, and it took her a minute to realize her mother was calling her in for supper.

"Are you okay, Sarah?" her mother asked, as Sarah toyed with her food. "Aren't you hungry? I hope you're not getting the flu. It's supposed to be bad this year. Maybe you should get a flu shot."

"No, Mom, I'm fine," Sarah said, taking a bite of omelette. She felt as if part of her was sitting at the table while the other part was back in the old synagogue. What would happen tomorrow when she lit the candles? Would she find out more about Wolf, Saraleh and their family?

She knew her mother was worried that she wasn't really fine, but she didn't know how to explain what she was feeling. This was like no dream she had ever had. She felt the dusty air of the other world in her throat. As she sipped some hot mint tea she began to feel more like herself, but she couldn't stop the thoughts racing around in her head. Her mother looked thoughtful too, even a bit sad, and on impulse, Sarah got up and gave her a big hug. "It'll be okay, Mom, you'll see," she said. She had no idea if she was right, but it was good to see her mother smile.

Third Day:

The next morning, Sarah jumped out of bed as soon as she woke up, sure that it would be a good day. Her grandparents were coming. The ship, the synagogue, the rabbi's words — all seemed far away as she helped her mother clean the house. Then her mother asked her to pick up a few things from the corner store. Brrr — it was freezing. Even though the sun was shining, Sarah was glad to be wearing the hand-knitted toque and gloves she'd bought at a small shop just down the road in Kensington Market. Her mother had told her that Great-Grandma Ruth's parents had owned a small grocery store in Kensington Market when they first settled in Toronto, but she didn't know if the store was still there. "Of course, most of the shops are so different now, I don't even think Grandma Ruth would remember which one it was," she had said. "But I was so happy to move back to this neighbourhood after all those years in the suburbs."

Sarah loved her family's old, red-brick house with its shady garden just north of College Street in the heart of the city. She wouldn't want to live anywhere else.

She hurried home with tea and milk, and a package of gingersnaps she'd grabbed off the shelf at the last minute.

Her grandma loved gingersnaps. She always looked forward to her grandparents' visits. They lived in an apartment in Richmond Hill, close to Toronto, so she got to see them pretty often. This was just as well, because they were the only grandparents she had. Her father's parents had been killed in a car accident when he was in university, before he'd met her mother. There was a picture of them on her father's desk; it showed a smiling young couple having a picnic on the beach. Her father said they had asked a fisherman to take the picture when they were on their honeymoon in Prince Edward Island. The man had even given them a fresh-caught lobster as a wedding present. "They would have loved you a lot," he'd told her once.

Thinking about presents reminded Sarah that she would get a special Hanukkah gift tonight. Her grandparents always gave her something wonderful when they came for their Hanukkah visit. Last year, it had been tickets to *The Nutcracker* for her grandmother and herself. The ballet told the story of a little girl's adventures during Christmas, and most of the characters were magical toys and enchanted creatures. Sarah remembered how Ben used to pore over the Christmas catalogues that came in the mail, as if the toys were magic. "Why can't we have Christmas?" he'd begged one year. "Santa would give me everything I want." Even Santa Claus, Sarah thought bitterly, couldn't have given him the one thing he wanted most.

Although she and Ben usually got little presents and Hanukkah *gelt*, chocolate coins wrapped in gold foil, on each night of the holiday, their parents would wait until the last night to give them each a special gift. This year, Sarah hadn't asked for anything. The way Mom and Dad were acting, they'd probably forgotten all about presents. She didn't know what to give them, either. But she knew her grandparents wouldn't forget.

Later that afternoon, as Sarah helped get food ready for the visit, her mother said, "I've been thinking ... maybe it's not such a good idea to keep on lighting the candles this year."

"Mom!" Sarah nearly dropped the plate she was drying. "Why not?"

"Well, your father's so upset ... it's the first year ... maybe next year will be different ..." Her voice trailed off.

"But Mom, I'm here, too!" Sarah blurted out. She couldn't stop the words now. "And I want the candles and the menorah. I want to keep things the way we've always had them." She couldn't believe her mother was doing this — treating her as if she didn't exist. It was bad enough that her father was making her feel that way.

It wasn't just their own family celebration and memories that were important to her. This holiday was something that linked them to people all over the world and back through time. Especially now with the menorah her great-grandmother had given them.

"I really want to light the candles," she said, her eyes filling with tears.

Her mother looked shaken. "Of course you do. And I do too. What was I thinking?" She gave Sarah a hug. "We'll go on with the holiday. But you know, things are never going to be the same as they were," she added softly.

"I know, Mom, but that doesn't mean we have to change everything."

She wondered if she should tell her mother about the "visions." But how could she explain them? They were more than a dream; it was like watching a play with a mysterious script that somehow involved her, a play she got to act in as well as watch. She would sound crazy if she tried to describe what she saw.

She took her mom's hand. "What will you tell Dad?" she asked.

"I'll tell him how much it means to you, and if he's still upset, he can go out for that half hour." Her mother sounded hopeful, but her eyes looked troubled as she turned to set out the snacks.

While she finished drying the dishes, Sarah thought about her dad. He always shut himself in his study upstairs. Dad broods, but Mom keeps busy, Sarah thought. She'd been busy ever since Ben's death, cleaning out his room, volunteering at school, going back to work part-time. She was hardly home any more. But the boxes and bags of Ben's things were still in the basement. Mom hadn't got around to giving them away — maybe some things were just too hard. Sometimes Sarah went downstairs to look inside the bags, burying her face in the clothes that still had Ben's familiar smell.

The doorbell startled Sarah out of her thoughts. Grandma and Grandpa were at the door and there were hugs and kisses all around. "Hi Grandma B. Hi Grandpa A," said Sarah when she could get a word in edgewise. Grandma's first name was Bea, short for Beatrice. When Sarah was little, she thought it was the letter B, so she called her "Grandma B." And then it was natural to call her grandfather, whose name was Albert, "Grandpa A." The names had stuck, and now everyone called them that.

"Where's Michael?" asked Grandma when they were all settled with cups of tea and hot cider, munching fancy pastries and Sarah's ginger cookies.

"He's working on some case notes," said her mother. "He'll be down for supper."

Her grandfather asked her about school, and Sarah, grateful for the change of topic, quickly began chattering about the poet who had visited and the songs they were rehearsing for the winter concert. Glancing out the window, she noticed that the short December day was nearly over. Soon it would be dark enough to light the Hanukkah candles. She wondered what to do if another vision came while her grandparents were there; she hadn't even thought about what would happen if other people were around. She couldn't just sit there "like a stuffed dummy," as Marnie would say. But Grandma B saved the day.

"Rachel, I'll help you with supper after the candles are lit. I'm sure your father would rather relax here in the living room with Sarah," she said. "Best to keep him out of the kitchen, anyway," she teased. "You know, we've been married over forty years, and I still have to show him how to boil water. But he's useful in other ways, aren't you, dear? Right now he misses summertime and taking care of his rose garden." Her grandfather shrugged and smiled at her. Grandma B was the talkative one. Grandpa A just liked to sit quietly and Sarah was sure he wouldn't mind if she seemed to do the same.

There were four candles today: three plus the *Shamas*. The array of colours looked prettier every day. They all said the blessing together as they lit the candles, then Grandma B took a small rectangular package wrapped in blue tissue paper out of her purse.

"Now for my surprise, Sarah," she said. "I hope you like this, darling," she said. Sarah didn't know what to expect. She opened the wrapping carefully and found a blue velvet box, the kind jewellery came in. Inside, nestled on a bed of cotton, was a round gold locket on a delicate gold chain. Sarah's name was engraved on the face of the locket in elegant letters, next to a tiny rose.

"It's beautiful, Gram," she cried.

Sarah had wanted a locket for months, ever since Marnie had got one for her birthday last spring. "Maybe you'll get a locket, too," Marnie had told her. "Then we can put each other's pictures inside." This was what best friends did, she assured Sarah. Now Sarah couldn't wait to show Marnie her new treasure.

"The locket was mine, darling, with the rose already engraved, and I had your name put on it," said her grandmother, as she watched Sarah hold the necklace up against her sweater. "Look inside," she added eagerly.

Sarah found the catch to open the locket. Inside she found a small — very small — photograph of Ben's face. She gasped. The picture had been cut from a larger photograph taken before he got sick.

"Oh my!" said Sarah's mother. Sarah couldn't tell if her voice was pleased or upset. Grandpa A gave her mother's hand a little pat. Everyone was watching her, waiting to see what she would do.

Sarah snapped the locket shut, fighting the urge to drop it on the floor and trample it. Ben, Ben, always Ben! Why was it always about him? And why did everyone have to keep reminding her of what had happened to him? She burst into tears. The next moment, she felt the locket fly out of her hands, into the air, onto the floor. She looked down at it, confused — she hadn't known she was going to throw it down like that.

"Oh dear. I'm so sorry. I just thought you'd like something to remember him by," said Grandma B.

"I told you, Bea," she heard Grandpa saying softly, and she felt her mother gently take hold of her shoulders.

"It's okay, Sarah," her mother whispered. Then, in a louder voice, "Come in the kitchen, Mama. Sarah will be all right with Dad."

The two women left the room, and Sarah looked tearfully at Grandpa A, who had settled back in his favourite armchair. He looked back at her calmly. He always had an unruffled air about him. Whenever Sarah got upset when she was little, he would do magic tricks to cheer her up. But now there were no tricks.

"You want to sit by me, honey?" he asked. The chair was almost big enough for two people.

Sarah shook her head, but then squeezed in next to him, anyway. He had a comfortable smell, wood smoke, freshly-ironed shirts and something more personal, more mysterious. She snuggled against his grey sweater, wetting it with her tears. "Sometimes you remember too much, eh?" he said.

As her sobs eased, she saw the candle flames flicker, even though the air was still. The hair on her arms prickled. She closed her eyes and let herself go into the darkness, wherever it would lead her.

Her nose twitched as an oily, fishy smell invaded her nostrils, followed by a jumble of other smells. She recognized the strong odour of pickles, the yeasty fragrance of bread baking and a pungent lemony scent like furniture polish that made her nose and the back of her throat tingle.

She opened her eyes to find herself standing just inside a door, next to a large glass window that let some cloudy light into the room. She looked around eagerly. Realizing she was completely alone, she decided to explore. A few wooden barrels, almost as tall as she was, stood like guards against one wall. Lifting the lids and peeking in, she found sardines in one — their strong, salty smell rising up to meet her — and fat pickles in another, floating in their own juice. On the wall opposite the barrels was a long wooden counter with an old-fashioned metal cash register; behind the counter were shelves crammed with boxes of sugar and salt, soap powder and clothespins and many other things. This must be a grocery store, she realized, even though it was nothing like the stores she knew in Toronto. A thick layer of sawdust covered the wooden floor, and there was no fancy packaging — all the colours seemed quieter somehow.

She didn't linger at the counter because her nose drew her towards an open display case in the back of the store. It was chock full of different kinds of breads and rolls, smelling freshly baked and yummy. She reached out to touch a bagel sprinkled with poppy seeds — it was still warm.

Sarah whirled around, startled, as a stern voice said, "Now, young lady, no eating between meals … well, one bagel," the voice relented. "How could it spoil your appetite? Especially a girl like you with chicken bones for arms."

The man seemed to have appeared from thin air. She was sure no one had come in through the front door. But then Sarah saw a blue brocade curtain hanging right at the back of the store — he must have come from behind that curtain. She was scared for a moment, but the voice was somehow familiar, and when she saw the man's red beard she realized that he was Wolf. What a relief! She was glad to see him, and by now not even surprised.

Wolf looked down at her from his great height; he was a lot taller than her father or her grandfather. He seemed puzzled to see her but not angry, and he smiled as he handed her the bagel. "Strange clothes you have on, little one," he said. "We hired you to help in our store, not come to a party. But now that you are here, Rosalie, let's find you some work to do."

He must have mistaken her for someone else, she thought, as she looked down at her clothes. She had put on a skirt today, an old plaid kilt of her mother's, and a blue-green wool sweater. I must look like I'm from another planet, she thought. She wondered how far back in time she was. Did these people even know about other planets? As she looked up at Wolf shyly, at a loss for words, the sound of a baby crying came from behind the curtain.

"Wait here a moment," Wolf told her. "I know something you can do." He disappeared back through the blue curtain as suddenly as he had entered.

Sarah took a bite of the bagel in her hand. It was much harder on her teeth than the bagels in Tim Hortons or even the ones from the bakery on Harbord Street near her house. It tasted salty and a little sour, and needed a lot of chewing. As she ate, she thought about all the fast-food places and stores in her own time, and realized in a flash why the colours seemed so muted here — there was no plastic!

She sat down on a wooden crate next to the long counter to finish her bagel. In a few minutes, Wolf returned, holding a little boy in his arms. If this was the same baby she had seen on the ship, Sarah thought, a whole year must have gone by; he looked that much older.

"Don't cry, *Tateleh*," Wolf murmured, then lowered the child gently into Sarah's arms. "Hold him for a while, Rosalie. He is sick and doesn't want to settle. Maybe a new face will make him happy while I sort these cheeses." He pointed to some wheels of cheese on the counter, the size and shape of large cakes but creamy in colour.

The little boy reached up to touch Sarah's long hair. "Good, he likes you," Wolf said. He looked at Sarah as if seeing her for the first time. "Come to think, you look a lot like my Saraleh, my oldest girl. Except for the hair — she has red hair like me." He started organizing the cheeses, continuing the conversation as he stacked them on the counter. "So many people are leaving the *shtetl,* coming to this new country. You have come from far away, too, I think."

Sarah could only nod. Really far away, she thought. Then, as Wolf seemed to be expecting an answer, she said truthfully, "I've only just arrived here."

"Did your family come straight to Toronto?" he asked. "Our ship landed in Halifax, but people from our village had already come to Toronto and made a community here, so we joined them. I think you will feel comfortable here. Already we are building a new synagogue, and this market is busy as a beehive. It is a good sign, a new beginning for so many families after all our wandering."

The little boy began to whimper. Wolf smiled as Sarah tried to distract the baby by making silly faces. It really was remarkable how much he looked like Ben had when he was little. He even smelled the same. They both had the same round cheeks and full lips. He's a baby, she told herself. That's how babies look.

But this little boy had blue veins showing through the clear skin of his forehead, like lines for rivers on a map, and his brown eyes had dark circles under them. As she held him, she saw purple-blue bruises on his legs, below the knees. Like Ben, last year. They'd thought Ben was just having a hard time adjusting to Grade 1: he seemed tired all the time, he had problems with reading, he got bruised from playing at recess. If only they'd known sooner what those signs really meant.

And suddenly it clicked — Sarah knew in a flash of certainty that the little boy in her arms had the same illness as Ben. "He's sick," Wolf had told her, with a worried look on his face. Her stomach did a little flip. What if … he did not get well? She knew that a hundred years ago many children died even from simple things like measles and the flu. They hadn't invented vaccines for those illnesses, and they certainly wouldn't have had the new medicines and technology that had kept Ben alive. Alive as long as possible, anyway.

Patricia, one of Ben's nurses at the Hospital for Sick Children, had explained to Sarah that leukemia was a disease of the blood, a kind of cancer of the blood cells. "We don't know what causes it, but there's a problem in the bone marrow," the nurse had said, "the soft centre of our bones where blood cells are made. Ben just doesn't have enough red blood cells to carry oxygen through the body — that's why he is so pale and doesn't have much energy. We need white blood cells to fight infections, and Ben doesn't have enough of those either, so he gets colds and sore throats easily. And all those bruises he gets are because he doesn't have the platelets that stop us from bleeding too much when we get a cut."

Sarah perched on the hard crate, remembering Patricia's

words and stroking the little boy's dark hair. His eyes were closed and he was relaxing into sleep. Wolf probably didn't even know how sick he really was. Maybe it's better not to know too much, she thought. The doctors had given them hope with Ben, but for what? Just to take it away again, like those dreams where the earth opens up and falls away underneath your feet. Maybe this little boy wouldn't have to go through the ordeals Ben had suffered.

The doctors had talked about doing surgery for Ben, replacing his bone marrow with marrow from someone healthy. Family members were the best donors, and Sarah was tested to see if her bone marrow would match Ben's. "It will grow back, just the way hair does and the way our bodies make more blood when we cut ourselves or give a blood donation," her father reassured her. She was scared of having an operation and had nightmares of huge needles and of her bones crumbling like old chalk, but she would have done anything to help Ben. But the surgery never happened. Her bone marrow didn't match and neither did her parents', and they didn't have any luck finding another donor.

One day while Sarah sat reading to Ben, he looked up at her and said, "I feel like there's a big slimy sea monster inside me, slurping me up."

"Ben, when did you ever see a sea monster?" she said, trying to make her voice cheerful.

"In my mind. You can't see a sea monster with your eyes, silly," Ben laughed. "He's got a long purple tongue that works like a straw. But he's really not so bad when you get to know him."

He stopped, a shadow passing over his face, then whispered urgently, "Don't tell Mom and Dad about him. Pretty please? Promise?" Sarah realized with a shock what he was really telling her — he could feel death inside and he was getting ready for it.

His eyes pleaded with her, and Sarah promised. And she couldn't break a promise, could she?

Only two weeks later, Ben died. He just shut his eyes and let out a big sigh while they were all together watching television one night. Sarah was glad that she and her parents were there with him, but it was still a terrible memory.

She tried not to think about that night, but it was like trying not to think about pink elephants when someone told you not to — you thought about them even more.

The child in her arms looked up at her suddenly with wide-open eyes, and said "Sarah? I'm thirsty." Then he fell back to sleep. He was asking for the other Sarah, his sister, but his words made Sarah shiver.

And yet this boy *wasn't* Ben, and his illness, whatever it was, wasn't hers to worry about. She looked over to the counter and Wolf straightened up from his work. "It is getting late," he said, glancing toward the window where the afternoon light was fading. "Here, taste this before you go." He handed her a thin sliver of pale yellow cheese. She took a bite; the cheese had a sharp, earthy taste. Sarah remembered Persephone from the Greek myth, the girl who ate six pomegranate seeds in the underworld and then had to live there for six months every year. Would she have to stay back here in time because she'd eaten a bagel and a piece of cheese?

"The boy is sleeping, Rosalie. You have done well." He touched her hair lightly. "In our village, the old women used to talk about healing hands. Only a few people are born with this gift, Rosalie." He paused. "It is a hard gift, like a stone you must carry, but a gift all the same."

Wolf began clearing space on the counter. "You must help me with one more thing before you go home," he said. "Could you set out boxes of candles for the start of Hanukkah?" He showed Sarah a stack of cardboard boxes behind the counter, and then scooped the sleeping child from her arms. "I will take the boy inside to his mother. Soon his sisters will come home from school, and they will help her take care of him."

Sarah was afraid Wolf would ask her why she wasn't in school, but he didn't say anything as he watched her arrange the boxes in a geometric pattern on the counter. The candles were all orange, in white cardboard boxes printed with Hebrew writing. Wolf reached out with one hand, still holding his son tight, and gave Sarah a box of candles. "Take these home to your mother, little one. Tell her you have worked well today." Then he went back through the blue curtain.

Sarah wondered what she should do now. She wanted to see Saraleh and the little sister, but she felt a wave of fatigue wash over her and settled back down on the wooden crate, waiting to see what would happen next. Not a minute had passed before Wolf reappeared. "I will put this here to go with the candles," he said, and set a shiny brass menorah on the counter, in the centre of Sarah's display. "Have a good Hanukkah, Rosalie," he said as he left again.

From the back room, she heard the sweet, silvery music of Wolf's harmonica, and a woman's voice singing. She stared at the gleaming menorah for a few moments; it looked familiar. Then she took a deep breath, savouring again all the aromas of the store. She felt herself getting drowsy … the smells and sounds began to drift away. The crate that had been so hard against her body now felt soft as a cushion.

Sarah found herself curled up in the armchair next to Grandpa A, who was fast asleep and snoring softly. The smoke from the candles in the menorah drifted upwards. All the candles were burnt out except for one tiny flame on the far right.

Then her mother appeared in the doorway to say that dinner was ready. Her father had come downstairs and was standing at the table, ladling soup into bright pottery bowls. "Soup of the evening, beeyoutiful soooup," he sang, smiling at Sarah. It was a line from an old nonsense poem he used to read to her. She smiled back, glad to see him in a good mood.

Grandpa A stretched, yawned and caught Sarah in a bear hug. "Do you feel better now, honey?" he asked. Strangely enough, she did. She picked up the locket, which someone had rescued from the floor and put on the coffee table beside her, and Grandpa A helped fasten it around her neck. The locket felt all right now. It was *hers*, and she could choose which picture to put inside. She opened it for a quick peek — even the photograph of Ben's face seemed happier.

She looked at the tiny rose carved on the locket's gold face and thought about the name Wolf had called her: Rosalie, a little rose. She thought about his words, too. But he was wrong about the healing hands. If it was true, why hadn't she been able to help Ben?

Something else was puzzling her. The idea had started at the store. She felt connected to the people she was meeting in the candles' light, as though they weren't characters in a dream or even a story but real-life people, people who had lived long ago, even before the time of Great-Grandma Ruth. They had a store in Kensington, just like her mother's family had, and there was a family resemblance … Could they really be her own ancestors? The possibilities made her head spin as she tumbled the idea over and over in her mind.

"Come on, sweetie," said Grandma B, interrupting her thoughts as she slid an arm around her shoulder. Sarah breathed in her light, flowery perfume contentedly. "My grandmother always said there's nothing so bad that a good bowl of hot soup won't make you feel better." So they went in to eat.

FOURTH DAY:

Monday, December 9

When Sarah woke up on Monday morning, the fog was so thick she could hardly see out the window. The weather matched her state of mind. Her experiences with the candles were getting so confusing that she had to talk to someone or she'd explode. But who? Not her mother or father, not her grandparents. She thought about her best friend Marnie, but then remembered the conversation they'd had last Saturday afternoon.

"Come on, Sarah," Marnie had said. "It's Christmastime … well, Hanukkah. Almost six months already. I'll bet Ben wouldn't want you to feel sad all the time. He was such a happy little guy."

Sarah had just shrugged awkwardly.

"I hate it when you're like this," Marnie said. "I know it's awful, but life has to go on."

What if it were you? Sarah thought. Even though Marnie was her best friend, she just didn't understand. And Sarah didn't think Marnie would understand about the menorah either, or the things she was seeing.

Who else could she tell? She thought about all the girls she hung out with at school, but shook her head. None of them would get it. Then she remembered Raphael — maybe he would understand what she was talking about. She'd known Raphael since kindergarten. He was one of those kids who never seemed to do anything wrong, and he was seriously into math and science, especially computers. Lucky for him he played a mean game of basketball, or he'd probably be a bit of a nerd, especially as he was really into outdoor stuff — hiking, camping, canoeing. None of the other guys were into any of that. Raphael was different, a little shy, especially after his parents got divorced a couple of years ago, but he knew a lot about things like UFOs and aliens. Maybe he'd be able to help her figure out the visions.

She remembered an amazing experience they'd had last spring during a field trip to a nature conservation area. The class had been looking for leaves and mushrooms and stuff for their science scavenger hunt, and she and Raphael had come across a mother deer and two fawns grazing in a shady clearing.

"Shhh," Raphael said. His face lit up. Sarah had never seen him look so happy.

They had stood spellbound behind some bushes, watching the beautiful creatures — until Marnie and Dave, the other members of their group, had come crashing along the path. They made so much noise that the deer ran away. Dave had cracked a stupid joke about Sarah and Raphael being alone together, and Raphael was so embarrassed that he didn't talk to her at school for almost a week. But Sarah had never forgotten the beauty of that moment with the deer.

Back at school after the summer, some kids had found it hard to approach her after they learned about her brother's death. But on the second day back, Raphael put a slightly wilted daisy on her desk and murmured, "I'm sorry about your brother." He was the only one who seemed to understand. Maybe it was because of his parents, she thought.

Of course, divorce wasn't the same as dying. Raphael lived with his mom but he still got to see his dad a lot. They went camping together in the summer like they used to, and Raphael would tell the class about paddling a canoe, seeing moose, otters and wolves, sleeping under the stars.

But she remembered how sad Raphael had been when his parents split up. Back in Grade 4, she'd thought that was the scariest, worst thing that could happen to anyone.

Sarah decided she would find a way to talk to Raphael at school that day. He was the only one of her friends who might believe her. She couldn't keep her secret any longer, or figure it out on her own.

Monday morning went by quickly, although she was so distracted Mr. Keats had to tell her a few times to pay attention. After lunch Sarah went over to the computer centre, where Raphael liked to hang out. Mr. Keats sometimes gave people permission to stay in at recess and work on computers.

"Hey, Raphael," said Sarah.

"Hey, yourself," he said.

"Whatcha doing?"

"Trying to beat this new game. If you do all the math problems right, you get to make up an action story."

"I'd rather just start with the story," Sarah said.

"Sure — but that's not the way to play the game," Raphael told her. "It would be like cheating. Anyway, math is fun."

"Well, it is for you. Guess I'll go outside." Sarah got up from her chair. Whatever had made her think she could talk to Raphael? Mr. Know-it-all, Mr. Perfect.

"Hey, Sarah, wait a minute." He turned to look at her. "Stick around. I could do the math part quickly so we can get to the story — I already know how to do most of these questions. My dad taught me," he added. "I mean, I'm not trying to show off or anything."

"Okay. I mean, sure," Sarah said.

They sat at the computer for a while making up a graphic story about space travel, looking for another world in the future. It gave Sarah a perfect opening to talk to Raphael about her problem.

"Raphael, what if we added a device for going back into the past?"

"You mean, like breaking through the time barrier in reverse? Very cool. We could go back to the dinosaurs, or even earlier." He clicked on the time icon. "Where do you want to go?"

Sarah thought a moment. "Raphael," she said, intending to choose her words carefully but then just blurting it out. "What if time travel isn't just a story people make up? Do you think it could ever be true?"

"In real life, you mean?'

"Well, sort of. Like going back in time, then coming forward again."

Raphael looked up from the computer, intrigued. "What are you getting at, Sarah?"

She didn't know what to say next.

"Come on. Tell me."

"Promise you won't tell anyone else?"

Raphael looked around the almost-empty room. "Okay ..."

Sarah hesitated, not sure whether to go on. Maybe Raphael would just think she was weird. But he looked at her thoughtfully, almost the way he'd looked while they were watching the deer, and encouraged her to continue. "What do you mean, Sarah?" he asked. "What's going on?"

Just then the bell rang and Mr. Keats came in. "All right, ladies and gentlemen, recess is over. The rest of the class will be coming in any minute, so tidy up and go back to your seats. Sarah, did I give you permission to stay in today?"

"It's okay, Mr. Keats, I was helping her with Math-Flick," said Raphael.

Sarah felt relieved but also annoyed with herself. She'd missed her chance to talk.

But Raphael didn't let it go. "Tell me later," he whispered as they went back to their seats.

After the last bell, Sarah headed home along College Street. The fog had lifted, and a pale sun shone through the clouds. She liked this walk, seeing all the different people, the stores and the old buildings. There was a woman who walked her cat on a leash every afternoon and always said hello to her, and today she passed a homeless person asking for change. She was just thinking how sad this was, especially in winter, when she heard Raphael behind her.

"Hey, Sarah, wait up!" She stopped and waited for him to catch up. "You can't just leave me hanging like that," he said with a grin. "What's all this about real-life time travel?"

When he said it like that, even Sarah thought it sounded a bit nuts. She was beginning to wish she'd never said anything at all.

"It's nothing, really …" she began.

But Raphael persisted. That was one thing about him, he didn't give up. "No, I don't think it's nothing. I think there's something you wanted to ask me … or tell me." They walked quietly together for a while before Raphael said, "Does it have to do with … I mean, how are you doing, Sarah? … About Ben, I mean."

"Okay," she said.

"That's what I said when anyone asked me about my mom and dad's divorce," Raphael told her. "But I felt pretty cut up inside. I didn't see why it had to happen."

"Yeah," Sarah admitted. "I feel bad all the time — and so do Mom and Dad, so I can't talk to them. It just makes it worse."

"That's exactly how I felt," said Raphael. "My parents were sad, but still mad at each other. So I never knew what to say. But they tried to be nice when I was around. And now it's not so bad."

"At least you get to see your dad. You get to see both of them," Sarah said, surprised at how bitter she sounded.

"Yeah — though sometimes it's hard going from house to house. And it was hard getting used to my dad's girlfriend, though she's okay. Now my mom's met someone, too, but he's a jerk …"

"I'd give anything if I could just see Ben one more time," Sarah said.

"Is that what you mean by time travel?" Raphael asked quietly.

"Not exactly. But I think it's connected somehow. Do you know about Hanukkah, Raphael?"

"Sure."

"Well, this year we're using my great-grandmother's old menorah," Sarah explained. "Her family brought it from Europe with them when they came to Canada. Maybe it's just a coincidence that it's the first Hanukkah after Ben … you know … but whenever I light the candles, I … things happen."

"What kind of things?"

"I see people, and it's like I'm in different places … on a ship, or an old synagogue in Russia somewhere. Last time it was a little grocery store right here in Toronto. It's not Egyptian or medieval times, just about a hundred years ago, and the people seem … familiar. Like they're my great-great-grandparents or something."

"Wow," breathed Raphael.

"In fact," Sarah went on, "I'm pretty sure they *are* my relatives, my ancestors." There, she'd said it out loud: the idea that had been haunting her since she'd visited Wolf's store. Now she was sure that Raphael would laugh at her or think she was completely out of her mind. And maybe she was.

Raphael kicked a can that was lying on the street. "That

is so cool," he said.

"It's not cool!" Sarah burst out. "And it's not like one of your science experiments. It's driving me crazy."

"Why?" Raphael asked, sounding genuinely surprised. They had stopped for a moment in front of an antique store. "I think it would be neat to see people from your past. They're not — hurting you or anything, are they?"

"No, nothing like that. But it's so confusing. There's a little boy who's sick, and he reminds me a lot of Ben. And his sister is named Sarah, too, and their father plays the harmonica; he's the one who runs the store."

"So you see where they live and all that?"

"Yes," Sarah said. She began to breathe easier. "When I was on the ship, I really was sailing in the middle of the ocean. And the store, well, it was so different from stores now. Even the food tasted different. The bagel was so chewy …"

"You got to taste things? Sweet!" They had reached the corner of Major Street. "We're almost at my house — my mom's house. Why don't you come in for a snack or something, and I'll ask if I can go over to your place."

Now Sarah was surprised. "Why do you want to come to my house?"

"Well, I want to be there when you light the candles. That's the only way I can get to see this happen, right? Do you think it would work for me?" he asked eagerly. "Or is it just you? Have your parents seen anything?"

Sarah explained that her parents and grandparents didn't know and she didn't want to tell them yet. And she didn't know if it would work for Raphael or not.

In fact, she didn't even know if she wanted Raphael to be part of this experience. She hadn't expected him to ask if he could come over — but, of course, she should have known he'd want to see it for himself. She felt torn; the visions were hers and made her feel special. But if someone else saw them too, she would feel less alone, less scared, and she'd be able to truly believe they were real. But would he see the same things she did?

They walked the next block in silence until they stopped at Raphael's house. Raphael's mother had just come home from work. She gave Sarah and Raphael some juice and cookies, and said there was no problem with him going over to Sarah's house. But not today, because Raphael had a dentist appointment. "Tomorrow would be fine, as long as it's okay with your mother," she said.

"Oh, yes, Mrs. Wilson, I'm sure it will be," Sarah said.

That night, when Sarah lit the candles, she touched the polished metal of the menorah wonderingly with her fingertips. What made it so magical? She thought of all the people who had handled it even before Great-Grandma Ruth. How old was it, anyway?

She had chosen four blue candles tonight with a yellow *Shamas*, shining like a star in a blue sky. The week before, a poet had come to give a special writing lesson to her class. The topic was "The Colours I Feel," and the poet asked them to write about things that they saw, heard, smelled, tasted and touched that corresponded to a favourite colour.

The sense of sight was easy, but the other senses were harder to describe. How does a colour sound, or smell, or taste, everyone wondered. The poet suggested they think about their own experiences and use their imaginations. "Maybe yellow is the smell of a lemon," she said, "or the sound of red is really loud, like a siren."

Sarah had chosen blue, a colour that made her feel happy and sad at the same time. People talked about the bluebird of happiness, but then they said you had "the blues" if you were upset. And her father liked blues music, where even the instruments sounded as if they were crying.

It was different from the music she and her friends liked, but sometimes Sarah would listen to it with her dad. He said it made sadness easier to live with. But he hadn't listened to the blues for a long time. Now he seemed to have such a huge hole of sadness inside him that nothing could fill it up. It seemed as big as the black holes in outer space that Mr. Keats had talked about in science class. Holes that would swallow you up if you got too close.

Sarah tried to think of happier music and she sang the Hanukkah song, *"Dreidel, dreidel, dreidel, I made it out of clay."* The year before, she had tried to make a clay *dreidel* for Ben but even after several attempts it didn't turn out right. The top couldn't spin and kept falling over. "Next year," her mother had told her. But now next year was this year, and there was no reason to make one. Sarah watched the candles flicker and burn lower, and the *Shamas* began to melt and drip wax onto the lions. Her parents were in the kitchen, talking quietly. Even if she'd had a *dreidel*, there was no one to play it with … she settled back on the couch in anticipation, her mind still spinning busily. Where would the menorah take her tonight?

❧

The couch began to feel hard and uneven. She found herself sitting on a cushioned chair, in an old-fashioned living room. The chair's velvety, dark purple cushions were lumpy and uncomfortable. Sarah looked around the room and saw a purple sofa and two more chairs, decorated with crocheted doilies. Frayed rugs covered the wooden floor, and a round pine table stood near the window. Peering through lacy patterns of frost on the windowpane, Sarah could see that it was evening. In the twilight she noticed some tree branches swaying in the wind and she realized this room was a few stories high, like the third floor of her own house. At the very top of the window was an oval of stained glass in a design of blue, green and amber. Lots of old houses on Sarah's street had stained glass windows, too, and she had often wished she had one in her room.

On the windowsill sat a lighted menorah holding four candles and the *Shamas*. The reflections of the flames danced on the frosty glass. This menorah was made of brass, polished until it shone, and decorated with two lions and a six-pointed star, something like the menorah that her great-grandmother had given them. In fact, it looked exactly like it. Was that just a coincidence — or another sign that these really could be her ancestors? She knew that even if this were only a vivid dream, her subconscious would most likely create her own menorah, the one she knew. Still, her heart jumped when she saw it, and she was even more convinced she was right: this was the actual past she was journeying to.

The menorah wasn't the only light in the room. The glow from a glass oil lamp on the table made the place look bright and cheerful. A little girl sat at the table by herself, spinning a *dreidel* in the light of the lamp. She was only about four or five, and instead of a skirt, she wore wide black bloomers that billowed out around her knees, and a matching black overblouse with long sleeves and a pointed collar trimmed with lace. She had a big white bow in her hair and black tights on her legs. The little girl was having trouble getting the *dreidel* to spin, but she kept practising determinedly.

Then a side door opened and two older girls came into the room. Sarah recognized Saraleh, though she looked several years older now than on the ship. The other girl was just a bit younger — probably she was the one who had been crying on the ship. She skipped over to the little girl at the table. "Here are the raisins and almonds that Papa gave us. Now we can all play," she said. They didn't have Smarties and pennies for tokens, the way Sarah and Ben used to.

"Hanukkah again," said Saraleh, giving each of them a handful of treats. "This time of year always reminds me of David. I still miss him after all this time, don't you, Mimi?" she said to the middle girl.

"Of course I do," she answered, spinning the top. It had four sides, with a different Hebrew letter printed on each one. When it landed, she read the letter facing upwards:

"*Shin* — oh, now I have to put something in." She took an almond from the little heap in front of her and added it to the pile in the centre of the table.

"I wish I'd known him," said the youngest girl. She spun the *dreidel* awkwardly. It made a few turns, then fell over. "*Hay* — that means I get some."

"Don't take all of it, Ruthie, just half," said Saraleh, seeing her scoop up the treats. "*Gimel's* for getting it all."

"And *nun's* for none, just like in English. I wish learning all of English was that easy," said Mimi, taking another turn.

The four letters on the *dreidel* were the first letters of the Hebrew words which meant, "A great miracle happened there," just as the rabbi had said.

"I still wish I'd known him," Ruthie repeated in a longing voice.

And Saraleh, spinning the *dreidel,* said dreamily, "I wonder what he's doing now."

The two girls looked at her sharply, and she added hurriedly, "I mean, I wonder what David would be doing if he were here."

"Probably just what we're doing — but he'd be stealing all the raisins," said Mimi, eating a few raisins herself.

"I guess so," Saraleh answered. "I wonder if they do anything, after … after … you know. Wherever they go. I wonder if he can see us, maybe."

The middle sister, Mimi, looked serious. "Sarah, you know Mama told us not to talk about that. She said it was bad luck." She spun the *dreidel.* "*Shin* again!" And she put in a few almonds.

Sarah wondered about David. Was he the little boy she had held during her visit to the store? It must have been him, and by the sound of it, she had guessed right about his sickness. Just like Ben, she thought, with a pang of sadness.

Sarah snapped out of her thoughts when, despite her warning to her sisters, Mimi herself began to talk about the boy. "If he were still alive, David would be getting ready for his Bar Mitzvah in a couple of years," she said. "You have his exact same eyes, Ruthie," she added, cupping the younger girl's face with her hands.

"Do I?" said Ruthie. "I wish we had a photograph of him."

"So do I, but all the pictures were lost in the fire," said Saraleh.

Fire? Sarah wondered. But she kept listening to the girls' conversation.

"You knew him," Ruthie persisted. "You can see him in your mind. I can't remember him at all." She spun the *dreidel* aimlessly and sighed. "I'm hungry," she added.

Saraleh stroked Ruthie's dark hair. "I wish we still lived right behind the store," she said. "Then I could get us some crackers and cheese just by going through the curtain. Now I'd have to go all the way down to the street. But anyway, Mama and Papa locked up the store when they went to the neighbourhood meeting, so we'll have to make do with these." She nibbled some of the raisins and almonds piled near her place at the table. "Mmm ... *rozhinkes mit mandlen*," she sang softly.

"And here's some of Mama's *mandelbrot*. I helped her make it," said Ruthie proudly, opening a tin box on the table and taking a cookie.

Sarah recognized the crunchy almond treats. They looked just the same as the ones she got from her favourite bakery on Harbord Street. But she thought sadly about what Mimi had said about David. Sarah realized she would never know what Ben might have done when he grew up. Would he have played hockey, studied medicine, trained to be an astronaut? What would he have looked like? And could he see her, now, wherever he was?

Sarah gave a little jump as the older girls stood up, abandoning the *dreidel* game. It was strange. She was close enough to touch them, but the girls didn't seem to be able to see her. "I'll fix your hair like I promised, Sarah," said Mimi. "Ruthie, you watch the candles. Be careful."

"They're almost burned out, she'll be all right," said Saraleh. She turned down the wick of the oil lamp to lower the flame and adjusted the position of the menorah so it sat more securely on the windowsill. "I remember packing this menorah when we left home," she said. "Mama said we had to bring it because her grandmother gave it to her when she got married. I wrapped it up in the lace tablecloth. It's travelled a long way, hasn't it?"

"Do you miss our old home, Saraleh?" asked Mimi.

"I guess I do. I remember our house and garden and I miss some of my friends, like Fagie. But it was dangerous too. I'm glad we live here now."

"I hardly remember anything," said Mimi. "Besides,

I can't imagine living in a little village like that, so old-fashioned. I just love it here."

The two older girls went into another room, and Ruthie, alone again, spun the *dreidel* around and around on the wooden tabletop, humming to herself as Sarah watched. This little girl's name was Ruth ... did she grow up to become Sarah's own Great-Grandma Ruth? She was so young, Sarah couldn't imagine her as the old woman they went to see in the nursing home.

"Ruthie," she said softly, but Ruthie just spun the *dreidel* again. "Can you hear me?" Sarah said, louder this time. The little girl reached out for an almond and popped it into her mouth.

Tonight it's like I'm invisible, Sarah thought, even though she could see and hear the girls and understand everything they said. What had changed? Sarah thought about books she'd read with time travel in them. The biggest problem was if someone went back to the past and altered something, it could change the whole future too. If Ruthie could see her now, what if she recognized her in the future? I'm not even born yet, thought Sarah. How confusing! Maybe the way it worked in these visions was that she couldn't be seen or heard if anyone there was still alive, like Great-Grandma Ruth.

Sarah swayed with dizziness from watching the *dreidel* spinning and twirling, or from the thoughts spinning inside her head. Ruthie nibbled some more of the raisins and almonds left on the table and spun the *dreidel* one more time. It danced over the polished wooden tabletop until it finally rolled over the edge. Ruthie picked it up, then, light as a little bird, she twirled her way across the floor and out the door to find her sisters. Sarah looked around the empty room, her gaze resting on the menorah — all the candles had burnt out. She stepped softly across to the table and reached for a couple of raisins and almonds, munching on them slowly. Then she turned down the wick of the oil lamp even further, until its flame, too, went out, and she sat back down on her lumpy chair.

She felt herself nod off for a moment, and when she opened her eyes, she was back in her living room, watching her own candles. The yellow *Shamas* was melted away, and the blue ones were burning low. Blue, she thought, remembering the poem she'd written at school.

She got up and rummaged for her writing folder in her backpack. She read over what she had written in the poetry lesson.

Blue is the sight of tears
the sound of blues music that my dad listens to
the smell of the ocean
the taste of blueberries

Tears weren't really blue but it sounded good, and made you think of water and feeling blue. She had got stuck on touch, but now she added:

Blue is the touch of my brother Ben's old baby blanket.

Grandma B and Grandpa A had given the fuzzy wool blanket to Ben when he was born. He'd slept with it when he was a baby and, when he was bigger, he'd carried it around everywhere. When he started kindergarten, Sarah's mother put the blanket away in her dresser, but Ben had demanded it again when he started getting sick. He had his blanket with him in the hospital, and right near the end, without telling anyone, Sarah had smuggled in a pair of scissors and cut off a little square of wool with its satin border. Ben was sleeping, but she knew he'd understand. She'd put the scrap in the top drawer of her dresser, tucked safely inside an old heart-shaped candy box she'd once got for Valentine's Day.

Every once in a while she took it out, whenever she remembered the times that she'd been cross with Ben. How guilty she felt when she thought of how often she'd even wished she didn't have a little brother. She knew that wishes couldn't make bad things happen, but sometimes in the middle of the night when she couldn't sleep, she wasn't so sure. That was when she took the little piece of blanket out of the box and held it next to her cheek — it made her connected to him somehow. The final glimpse Sarah had of Ben was seeing him in the white box with his blue blanket tucked around him. He looked so small and cold. She hoped the blanket was keeping him warm.

As Sarah read over her poem, she thought of another line:

Blue is the sight of Hanukkah candles burning, happy and sad at the same time.

The last candle sputtered out. She put away her writing and turned to her math homework. She was pretty sure she could figure out the answers to those problems.

Fifth Day:

Sarah couldn't believe the piles of clothing and stuff on the living-room floor!

Had her mother forgotten that Raphael was coming home after school with her today? Sarah didn't want him to see their house in such chaos. She hadn't explained the real reason for Raphael's interest, just said that he wanted to see their Hanukkah ceremony.

"I'm sorry," said her mother, her voice sounding distracted as she knelt on the carpet, sorting through the mess. "I got home from work early, and it seemed a good time to get all this stuff up from the basement. It's for charity ..."

"That's okay, Mrs. Goldman. It looks kind of like my room," Raphael said with a grin. "My mom is always telling me to clean it up."

How did he know just the right thing to say? Sarah wondered if he was this nice to his own mother.

She saw some old sweaters she'd grown out of in one pile; there was no one else in the family to hand them down to. Then she noticed the jumble of Ben's clothing — shirts, jeans, pajamas, all with empty arms and legs. There was even a little Toronto Blue Jays backpack with the price tag still on.

Sarah and Raphael sat down on the floor to help her mother fold the clothes and pack them in green plastic bags. Some of the clothes had been handed down from older cousins and friends. The menorah was a hand-me-down too, Sarah thought, but it was different from clothing — she would never give it away except to her own grandchildren, if she ever had any. Life was like a chain of handing things down, she thought, so many people living before her, so many to come afterward ...

"Do we have any photographs of our relatives before Grandpa B and Grandma A?" she asked her mother.

"No, we don't. I think there were some pictures, but they were all burned in a fire one time. Remember I told you that your great-great-grandparents had a store in the old Kensington Market? Well, they lived in the back, and one night the kerosene lamp tipped over and the kitchen curtains caught fire."

Sarah gasped.

"They all managed to get out alive," her mother went on. "My grandmother was only a baby, but the story goes that her father carried them all out into the snow. He even put galoshes from the store on her sisters' feet. The galoshes were too big — they were men's sizes — but at least their feet didn't freeze."

Sarah pictured Wolf's strong arms and broad back, and knew he could keep everyone safe.

"They had to move to a new place, but they still ran the store. And they managed to save the menorah. Most of the old family stuff was lost, though," her mother said, "even the pictures of their son who ... had been sick. He would have been — let me see — your great-great uncle, Sarah." Sarah's mother ran a hand across her forehead. "I'd forgotten about him," she added. "I haven't thought about any of this for a long time."

With a shiver, Sarah remembered the girls talking about the fire and the lost photographs while playing *dreidel*.

"Maybe there's a curse on our family," her mother said, a catch in her voice.

"No, Mom, no!" Sarah got up and hugged her mother, right in the middle of the bags of old clothes.

Raphael looked down at the faded pair of jeans in his hands. "The Egyptians used to believe in curses," he began in that know-it-all tone ... then his voice faltered. "But I don't," he continued. "People just run into bad luck sometimes. All that stuff about walking under a ladder or crossing the path of a black cat is just superstition."

"Of course you're right Raphael," said Sarah's mother. "I was just being silly." She stood up and brushed off her hands. "Listen, why don't I make you guys some sandwiches and milk, then it will be time to light the candles. I have to run a couple of errands, Sarah, so you two might as well just eat without me. I'll have something when I come home, and your father has a dinner meeting at the hospital so he'll be late."

"Wait, Mom, don't we have pictures even from after the fire?" Sarah asked, before her mother could leave the room.

"I don't think so. I think your great-great-grandmother

got superstitious — she thought taking photographs would bring bad luck. They said she got ideas like that sometimes. She didn't have you around, Raphael, to set her straight." She smiled at him. "And of course, most people didn't own cameras back then. They'd go to a photo studio if they wanted pictures on special occasions."

Her mother went into the kitchen, and Sarah and Raphael turned back to the pile of clothes.

"Hey, what's this?" exclaimed Raphael, reaching for a strand of gold ribbon that gleamed underneath an old raincoat.

"Let me see that!" cried Sarah. She had a sinking feeling in her stomach. Digging quickly through the floppy garments, she found it — furry arms, legs, ears, tummy: Ben's old teddy bear, Zachary. His honey-coloured glass eyes looked at her reproachfully, but he still grinned his silly stitched-on smile, as if someone had just told him a joke. He had a soft beanbag body, chocolate brown, with joints at the elbows and knees so his limbs could move easily. Around his neck, as if he were an Olympic champion, looped a wide gold ribbon with a medal attached.

Oh, no! Sarah thought. She can't do this to you, Zachary! She didn't want the bear pawed over by people in Value Village, even if it was for a good cause and would make some other child happy.

"It's Zachary, my brother's old teddy bear," Sarah explained to Raphael. "I couldn't *bear* it if they gave him away." She smiled weakly at her bad joke. "Here — why don't you take him?"

"Me? You should keep him, Sarah. Why don't you just put him in your room?"

"You saw how she threw him away in this pile. If she finds him again — I don't know what she'd do. She'd probably cry, and my dad would get mad at me. I can't deal with that right now. Maybe you could take Zachary for a while — like a visit — then give him back to me after the holidays. I'll figure out something by then."

"Sure," said Raphael, "That's cool with me." He put the bear in his backpack before they headed into the kitchen to eat their grilled cheese sandwiches.

"I'll be back in a minute," Sarah's mother said, going back to the living room. Sarah thought she was still puttering around with the clothes, but she returned to the kitchen holding a black and white photograph, its edges worn.

"Look," she said, "I found this in an old album. It's a picture of my grandmother with Grandma B and me, on my tenth birthday. Grandma B is my mother," she explained to Raphael.

She sat down and looked closely at the picture, touching it gently. "My grandma was always sweet to me," she said. "Sometimes she'd travel with Grandpa on business, but their house was near ours and we saw her almost every day when she was home. They owned a piano and she was my first piano teacher. She was a strict teacher, even though she was usually so easygoing. She made me play the notes over and over until I got them right. 'No use doing things half-hearted,' she used to say."

As her mother talked, Sarah and Raphael examined the

figures in the photograph. There was a small woman with frizzy hair, bright eyes and a determined expression. That would be Great-Grandma Ruth. Grandma B was wearing a fancy scarf and looked young and pretty. And Mom, well, Mom was younger than Sarah was now, kind of skinny, with an impatient expression on her face. They were sitting on the porch of a house which Sarah did not recognize.

"I hated to sit still back then," Sarah's mother continued. "But I did like listening to my grandma play the piano. Sometimes I made mistakes on purpose, just to hear her play the piece and show me how to get it right. She made it seem so easy." She smiled, and Sarah smiled back.

"Oh, well," said her mother, "those times are long gone now. Grandma Ruth had real talent, but it was much harder for women back then to be successful musicians or artists and still have a family. So she just played for herself, and taught me and a couple of my friends." She pinned the picture to the kitchen bulletin board.

Sarah cleared the dishes and then set up the menorah on the kitchen table. "I'm glad you want to join us for the holiday," her mother said to Raphael. Sarah told Raphael the words of the prayer, and he stumbled through it with her as she lit the candles. "Here, you can light the last one," she told him, handing him the *Shamas*. He held it carefully and lit the red candle, number five. A drop of green wax fell on his thumb as he gave the *Shamas* back to Sarah, and he peeled it off.

"Don't burn the house down," said her mother in a joking tone of voice as she headed toward the door. "I'll be back in an hour or so. I've got my cell phone, so call if you need anything."

When they were alone, Raphael turned to Sarah and said, "I was wondering …"

"What?" she prompted, when he didn't go on.

"Well, how can you be sure you're really going back in time? What if — if it's just your imagination or something?"

Sarah didn't know how to answer. How could she get him to believe her? Even she didn't know *why* she knew this was real. She was too mixed-up to speak, and she bit her lip as Raphael studied her face carefully.

"Never mind," he said. "There's obviously something strange going on." He touched the menorah gently and the candles jiggled a little. "I don't understand how this works, but I believe what you're telling me. So what do we have to do? Do we say anything special?"

"Like abracadabra?" asked Sarah in a teasing voice. "No, we just sit and look at it. Maybe it won't even work with a stranger here."

"Thanks a lot," said Raphael, rolling his eyes.

"Sorry. But I really don't know what will happen." She knew Raphael took her seriously, but his words still stung a bit. "Here, have a piece of Hanukkah *gelt*." From the package on the table, she handed him a chocolate coin and took one for herself. They sat there at the kitchen table and watched the flames as the chocolate melted slowly in their mouths.

Sarah shut her eyes for a minute, drifting, and when she opened them she was standing near the stove in a big, but cozy, kitchen. It looked different from her kitchen at home and all the kitchens she knew. There were no shiny appliances, no microwaves or toaster ovens, not even a gleaming refrigerator. The stove was made of heavy dark metal and radiated a delicious warmth. As she moved closer, she almost tripped over a stack of wood heaped on the floor. There was an opening on top of the stove where you could load the wood to make a fire. This stove wasn't only meant for cooking, it was there to warm the house all day. A kettle of water sat on top of the stove, bubbling softly. On the far side of the stove there hung a familiar blue curtain. Sarah remembered the curtain in the grocery store, and she guessed that she was back in the store again but on the other side of the curtain in the family's living space.

Looking through the window, Sarah could see that it was early evening. Clouds scudded through the sky and snowflakes swirled against the glass, blurring the world outside. On the windowsill, looking especially bright against the snow, was a menorah with five lighted candles, six with the *Shamas*. Like the one she had seen last night, it had a crown and two lions guarding the candles. Like that one and the one she had seen in the grocery store, it looked the same as hers. She was more and more certain now that it *was* hers.

As her eyes got used to the dim light in the room, Sarah

saw a round table with a few chairs around it. A kerosene lamp on the table cast a small, golden glow. Suddenly, a slight rustle at the table made Sarah realize that she was not alone. A woman was sitting there, huddled in a heavy shawl, so still that she looked like a shadow.

The woman made no sign that she had seen Sarah. Maybe she would be invisible tonight, the way she had been the night before. Then she heard muffled sobbing and realized the woman was crying softly, holding her head in her hands, lost in her own world.

At the sound of voices from beyond the curtain, Sarah stepped back into the shadows beside the stove. Wolf came into the room accompanied by Saraleh and Mimi. The two girls looked younger tonight than they had during the *dreidel* game, and the youngest girl, Ruth, wasn't there at all.

Wolf and the two girls sat down at the table, and Sarah shrank further into her corner, not sure if she wanted to be seen or not. This reminded her of times when she sat on the stairs at home, listening to her mother and father talking, wanting to hear and not wanting to at the same time, and certainly not wanting to go back to bed.

Wolf was trying to comfort his wife. "We have to be strong, Anna."

"David, my David," the woman said through her tears.

"You still have me and Mimi," said Saraleh. She and her sister were wearing long dark blue dresses and button-up shoes, the kind that would be expensive now in a "collectibles" shop. She got up to fetch a plate of small cakes from the counter, set the plate on the table, then sat down again quietly when her mother didn't look up.

"Anna," said Wolf gently, putting his arm around her. "Don't cry. There can still be more babies. Think of that."

Sarah bit her lip as she realized what was happening. This must be after the baby David died. She thought of Ben, and the raw grief welled up again in her heart. She struggled to hold in her tears as Anna raised her head to speak.

"If only we had been able to help him," Anna said. "I know it's been over a month already, but I can't stop wishing …" Sarah remembered all the "if only's" she'd thought about Ben, and before she could stop herself, she had stepped out from her hiding place.

"My brother Benjamin died, too," she whispered, moving right over next to Anna. Up close she could see traces of tears on the woman's face. Anna took her hand, and Sarah breathed a sigh of relief. She was glad that tonight she could be seen and heard.

"Who are you, little one, little *maydela,* and how did you come here?" Anna asked.

Sarah didn't know what to say; as she struggled for words, Wolf said: "I think this is the girl who is going to work in the store. She was supposed to come after lunch."

Wolf did not seem to remember her or the time she'd worked in the store and comforted David. Must be another time travel rule, Sarah thought.

"I'm sorry I'm late," she said. "I came into the store and didn't see anyone, then I heard voices and came back here. I didn't mean to interrupt."

"No, no," said Anna. "But you have come at a sad time,

even though the *Shiveh* is over. They say everything grows bigger with time except grief — but grief doesn't disappear so quickly, either." She turned to Wolf. "Maybe if we'd had better medicine …" she began.

"You know there was nothing we could do. We can't question what happens in life," Wolf said, but his eyes were troubled.

"Yes, we can!" Anna shouted suddenly. "Sometimes we must question!" She let out a piercing cry and flailed her arms in front of her, sweeping the blue and white plate of food right off the table. It shattered on the floor, scattering pastries, crumbs and shards of china. The girls turned pale and even Wolf looked scared. Sarah stood frozen, not daring to move.

As if that wasn't enough, Anna leapt up from her chair, shaking her head wildly — and all at once her hair came right off her head, dark curls flying through the air!

Sarah could hardly believe her eyes. Could hair fall off your head just like that? Underneath the curls, Anna's head was covered with short, badly-cut hair, the colour of straw, reminding her of Ben and other kids whose hair fell out because of chemotherapy treatments.

But seeing her curls lying on the floor, next to the smashed plate, seemed to bring Anna back to herself. "So, what is everyone looking at?" she said. "The world hasn't come to an end." She bent down, picked up her hair, and smoothed it back on her head. It was only a wig. Sarah almost laughed out loud with relief. How could she have thought real hair could just pop off someone's head? Strange things were happening, but not *that* strange. Of course Anna would be wearing a wig. That was the traditional custom for Jewish women after they got married. Not that many women did that anymore.

"These *sheitels*" said Anna, flicking stray hairs on her wig back into place, "They're not made for such commotion!"

Anna smiled then, a smile that lit up her whole face. "I feel better now," she said. "Sometimes feelings have to jump out like that, just like the wig jumped off my head. It's true, we still have each other. We will live through this together." She sat down heavily, and reached out to give each of her daughters a hug. "Mimi, sweep the floor for me, carefully now, before you cut yourselves," Anna admonished.

Mimi got busy, using a wooden broom with straw bristles. Saraleh held the dustpan for her.

"Now Papa, please bring me a glass of tea. And some more *rugelah* from that tin box on the shelf. It's Hanukkah, the candles are lit, we'll sit and have a bite to eat. Nothing is so bad that something good to eat won't help us feel better." Sarah remembered Grandma B saying the same thing the other night. Grandma B's grandmother, she realized, would be Anna. She could picture Grandma B as a little girl listening to her own grandmother.

Wolf lifted a teapot from the counter and poured some tea into a glass set in a metal holder.

"Anna," he said. He looked as though he wanted to say more, but he didn't.

Anna stirred in a spoonful of cherry jam from a bowl that

Saraleh brought to the table and sipped her drink quietly. *Glasses* of tea, not mugs or cups, and *jam* as a sweetener instead of sugar: everything was familiar but different. Mimi carried over a tin box with a label that said it contained rice, but when Anna opened the lid, Sarah could see it was filled with the delicious little pastries called *rugelah*. Sarah's mom always got *rugelah* at the bakery, along with *mandelbrot*, but these looked homemade.

The floor was now as clean as if the plate had never broken and the whole room felt different, more at ease. It was as if the room itself had taken a deep breath and then let it out in a huge sigh. The girls were munching *rugelah*, talking quietly, and Wolf was standing near the stove, playing a soft melody on his harmonica. Sarah wondered if her mother ever felt like screaming the way Anna had done, breaking plates and making noise, letting her feelings "jump out." Maybe Mom would feel better, too, if she did that. Maybe everyone would.

Anna pulled out the chair beside her and took Sarah's arm. "Sit, sit," she said. "Where is your family from, child?" Without waiting for an answer, she went on speaking: "We are all new in this neighbourhood, coming from somewhere else," she said, adjusting her wig again. "Czechoslovakia, Hungary, Romania, Poland, Russia. So many new people. So many different ways of talking. But we are all family here on this street."

Sarah was amazed at the way these people accepted her. Maybe, as Anna said, it was how they welcomed every new person into the neighbourhood. As immigrants, they all had things in common. But she was sure that she had a special reason to belong here, and that this was her own family, even though they had no idea who *she* was.

Saraleh offered her a *rugelah* and gave her a long, searching look. They smiled shyly at each other, and Sarah took a bite of the pastry — it was delicious. "You look familiar, somehow," said Saraleh. "Have we met before? Maybe I've seen you at school or on the street."

"Maybe," said Sarah, taking another bite of *rugelah*. Just like Wolf, she thought, Saraleh obviously doesn't remember me from before.

Sarah thought about her full name, Sarah Anne. In Jewish tradition, it was bad luck to name children after anyone still living; on the other hand, it was good luck, like a blessing, to give a new baby the name of someone who had died. That way, your love for that person would go on and on and their name would be remembered. Her mother had once told her that she'd been named for her great-great-grandmother and for a great-aunt who had died young. Anna must be that great-great-grandmother, which would make Saraleh her great-aunt … who would die young! What was going to happen to her? Sarah hadn't given it much thought before but decided she would ask her mom for the whole story.

"Losing a child is hard for women," Anna was saying, breaking into Sarah's reverie. "Hard for men, too, but harder for women. Men have work, books, *Torah* study, but we sit and cry and tell stories. Maybe men should cry more, too, who knows?"

"God works in mysterious ways," Wolf answered.

"Remember the story of Job. Who are we to question?…" he began again. Then he sighed. "It is hard for men, too, Anna."

Saraleh whispered, "Where did you get your clothes? Mama always says not to be rude, but they're so different — you wear pants, like a boy!" Sarah looked down at her denim jeans and baggy blue sweater. At least the sweater was hand-knitted wool, something these girls would know about. But the jeans — how could she explain them?

"I guess it does look strange. I come from really far away," she said. "But I do want to be your friend. And your sister's."

"Tell her your names, girls; make friends," Anna prompted.

"I'm called Sarah," said the other girl.

"And I'm Mimi. It's really Miriam, but everyone calls me Mimi. Mama says that sounds more Canadian," said the younger girl. "I'm working really hard at learning English."

"And what is your name, please?" asked Saraleh.

Sarah didn't want to tell them that she was also called Sarah. "Rosalie," she answered. It was the first name she thought of, the name Wolf had called her when he thought she'd come to help in the store. She liked the sound of it; it could be a name she chose for herself. Her own special name.

"Rosalie. It sounds pretty, like roses," said Mimi.

"Welcome to our home, Rosalie," Wolf said.

Anna went on with her own train of thought. "If we have another baby, a girl, we will call her Ruth after my grandmother. She was a good woman. And Ruth in the Bible was a loving friend and companion. Yes, a good name. And if it is another boy ..." her face clouded, then she went on. "I know ... we'll call him Joseph."

"Joseph," said Wolf, stroking his red beard. "But there is no Joseph in our families."

"That's true, but Joseph in the *Torah* told stories about dreams, didn't he? I think dreams send us messages from the other world, things we need to know. I didn't tell you, Papa, but I had a dream last night. I don't remember it all, but I think it meant good luck for our family. I dreamed about our menorah, all lit up with candles, in a big modern city like Minsk or Moscow or this Toronto but even bigger, with tall buildings and many people. And there were two children lighting it, a girl and a boy. I think they will be part of our family in times to come."

"Dreams," said Wolf. "You put too much faith in dreams, Anna. But Joseph it will be, God willing."

Sarah remembered all those times she'd heard Grandma B talk about how her mother Ruth was "the baby of the family," much younger than her two sisters. The previous night's visit, when she saw all three girls together, must have been several years later than tonight, long after David's death, the fire and the family's move to another house.

Her own visions, like dreams, worked in strange ways, Sarah thought. Time was all mixed up, not a straight line like days on the calendar. Memories worked like that, too — sometimes she remembered Ben when he was sick and sometimes when he was a little baby.

Sarah noticed the candles burning low in the menorah on the kitchen windowsill. Two of the flames shone brightly and then sputtered out.

"It's getting late, I'd better be going," Sarah said. She didn't want to disappear right in front of them. Maybe I can walk out the door, like I'm just going down the street, and then go back to my own time. Or maybe, she thought, I can just stay here and never go back at all. Anna gave her a big hug goodbye, and Sarah felt so comfortable pressed against her warm arms and pillowy fragrant bosom that she never wanted to move again. Maybe no one would miss her if she stayed.

"Come back soon," said Anna. "You are welcome in our house any time. And give your mother my *mitgefil*, my condolences, for your brother. Tell her women understand these things.

"And tell her to come buy her groceries from our store. Everything is good quality, and we'll give her a good price. Here, take another *rugelah* for Hanukkah," she added, holding out the tin of wonderful crescent-shaped, jam-filled cookies. She insisted that Sarah take two, then passed the tin to Mimi.

Wolf took Sarah by the hand and pulled back the curtain. "Come, I will take you out through the store." She had to leave, after all.

"Goodbye, Happy Hanukkah," Sarah called as they let the curtain fall behind them. She and Wolf walked through the store. "Walk with care, the streets are growing dark and icy. Go home safe," Wolf said. Sarah thanked him and slipped quickly out the door, away from the appetizing smells of baking and pickles. A little bell tinkled above the door as it opened and closed behind her.

As soon as she stepped outside onto the crowded street, she felt a blast of cold air. Snow swirled around her in the gathering dusk. Peering through the snow, she saw the glass windows of more shops along the street. Chickens and rabbits were hanging in one window, pots and pans stacked neatly in another. She heard a sharp whinnying, and, turning toward the sound, saw beside her a small grey horse harnessed to an open cart heaped high with rags and old clothes. The horse was pawing at the street, and his breath came out in a cloud of warm steam. Sarah stroked his soft, dappled coat; the animal barely twitched his ears. He seemed used to people touching him.

Then the street seemed to melt under her feet, and the snow blinded her.

🌿

Next thing Sarah knew, she was back at her own kitchen table. Raphael was still sitting across from her, staring at the last smoke from the candles. He looked dreamy, in his own world. Sarah was fine with that — she wanted to linger with her own memories of Anna's fierce outburst and warm embrace. But she wondered what he had seen in the candlelight.

Just then her mother came into the room, jolting Sarah and Raphael back to the present. "Hi, honey, I'm back. And

I brought some *rugelah* for you, I know you like them." She offered the paper bag to Raphael, then to Sarah.

When Sarah took a bite, she tasted jam, spice, honey and something delicious and faraway, yet familiar. Very familiar.

Raphael devoured his *rugelah* and asked for another.

"Help yourself, Raphael, then Sarah and I will walk you home. I know it's only a few blocks but it's getting late."

"It's okay — I'm going to my dad's tonight," Raphael said. "He asked me to call him and he'll pick me up. He lives near High Park, too far to walk. May I use your phone, please?"

Sarah stood next to him while he spoke to his dad. When he hung up she said, "Well? Did you see anything?"

"Wow, Sarah. You were right. I'll never doubt you again. It was amazing. It was … Thank you for letting me come over. I mean, wow! We've got to talk about this, but my dad will be here any minute. Let's meet up tomorrow."

Sarah felt a rush of relief — and excitement. Raphael *had* seen something. It wasn't all in her head. If she hadn't still been so caught up in her own experience, she would have insisted that Raphael talk to her right then and there. But she just said, "Okay — but promise you'll tell me."

Soon his father rang the doorbell, a tall man wearing a leather jacket. "Thanks for giving Raph a taste of something new," he said, smiling at Sarah and her mother.

Raphael gave her shoulder a quick pat — more like a flick of his hand — as he left. "See you tomorrow, Sarah." He was nearly as tall as his dad, Sarah noticed, as she watched him glide down the porch steps. He moved lightly, like the deer they had seen in the clearing.

After waving goodbye, she went up to her room to get ready for bed and found a lump under the covers, with Zachary's brown ear poking out. Raphael must have put him there, probably when he'd gone to the washroom before they had their sandwiches. Although it was silly, tears welled up in her eyes. She was glad Raphael hadn't taken the bear home, after all. And he'd even found a way to surprise her. She'd keep Zachary safe in her room so he wouldn't have to go to Value Village.

Sarah curled up in bed in her favourite flannel nightie. As she lay there, holding the bear close, she heard Anna's comforting voice, "We still have each other." But Anna had also said that sometimes we have to question things that happen in life. Before she could go on thinking about her own questions, the warmth of her bed drew her deep into sleep.

Sixth Day:

Sarah woke up early, in a hurry to get to school and talk to Raphael, but when she got downstairs, she found her father in the kitchen, making cinnamon buns. They were the frozen kind but still delicious, a family favourite.

"Mmm, smells great, Dad," Sarah said.

"Your mom had an early meeting today," her father said, sliding a pan into the oven, "so I'm on breakfast duty."

Wednesday was her father's day off from his medical practice, and one of her mother's days to go to work. Three days a week, she taught music and recreation at a senior citizens' centre and children's piano lessons at the Royal Conservatory of Music, a huge brick building downtown that looked like a castle. When Sarah visited her there, she loved to listen to the sounds of different instruments drifting like ghost music all over the building. Students practising, her mother said.

They had a piano at home, but her mother hadn't played much recently. When she was little, Sarah used to fall asleep listening to her mother play. She'd especially liked a French piece called "Clair de Lune." "Goodnight, Moon," she would whisper, looking at the moon outside her bedroom window and repeating the words from an old picture book. "Goodnight, cow jumping over the moon."

Her mother had tried to teach Sarah to play the piano, but Sarah didn't have the patience to practise. She got frustrated when she couldn't get the notes right the first time, and then she and her mother would argue. And her mother played so well Sarah felt stupid trying to learn. Sarah had been surprised to hear that her mother had felt the same way when her grandmother was teaching her. Maybe they had more in common than she'd thought.

Sarah didn't think she'd want to study medicine like her father. She couldn't handle being around all those sick people, especially if she couldn't help them get better. She remembered that when Ben first got sick, she had believed that her father would know exactly what to do, even though he was a family doctor at a clinic and not a specialist. When she'd realized he couldn't do anything, she'd secretly wished her dad had been a better doctor. Now she realized how much it must have hurt him, not to be able to cure his own son.

While she was waiting for the cinnamon buns to finish baking, Sarah wandered into the living room and sat down at the piano. Looking through the sheets of music, she found "Clair de Lune" and started picking out some of the notes. She did okay with the familiar melody, choppy and a few off notes, but still pretty. Maybe she would go back to learning piano some day.

She didn't hear her father come into the room, and his

voice startled her. "I thought I heard someone playing." Sarah looked at him carefully, trying to figure out what kind of mood he was in. In the past, it didn't matter if he was in a bad mood once in a while because he always got over it quickly, joking that he could have a hot temper even in a blizzard. But now, she never knew what might set him off or how long he'd stay mad. He was like the Native mask in *False Face,* the book she was reading. One side of its painted face was happy, one was scary, and you never knew which one would be in control. Sarah's hands hovered over the piano keys as she tried to remember if her father had told her not to make noise and she'd forgotten.

"Go on, it's nice to hear you playing again," he said. Phew, she thought. His happy face was showing, like the other night when he'd served the soup. He listened to her play for a few more minutes, and when she finished the piece for the second time, he went over and gave her a little hug.

"Come on. I think those cinnamon buns are just about ready," he said. She smelled cinnamon wafting into the room. Her mouth watering, she went to join her father as he lifted the pan out of the oven and cut carefully around the warm rolls with a spatula. He slid a few onto a blue plate and offered it to Sarah with a flourish.

She picked up one of the buns and blew on it to cool the gooey sugar glaze. Her father took a bun, too, then poured each of them a cup of coffee, adding lots of milk and a heaping spoonful of sugar to hers, just the way she liked it. This was a good sign, their special treat. They ate in companionable silence for a while.

Sarah told herself not to mention the menorah or anything connected with Hanukkah. It was nice being with Dad and she didn't want to upset him. But maybe there was one thing she could ask.

"Dad," she began, "do you believe in magic?"

"You mean, like rabbits jumping out of hats? Or guessing which card you're holding?"

"No, I mean real magic — like things that have special powers. Old masks that come to life, or special rings, or … stuff like that?"

"In stories, maybe," he said. "I guess people like to imagine things like that, but it doesn't happen in real life. Why — did you find a magic lamp or something?" he asked with a teasing laugh.

Sarah shrugged. "Just wondering."

Her father sipped his coffee.

"These buns are awesome," Sarah said, taking another one.

"Yes, they are," her father smiled. "I haven't made them for a while, have I?"

Impulsively, Sarah got up and gave her father a sticky hug. His flannel shirt felt soft against her cheek. He seemed so relaxed, she decided to take a chance. "Great-Grandma Ruth's menorah feels like magic sometimes," she said. "When the candles are lit, I see … places. And people. I don't understand it, Dad."

He pulled back to look her in the face. "We all have lots of people and places in our minds, Sarah. Pictures we don't even know about. They might come in dreams or when we're staring at the waves of the ocean or watching a fire burn — even a small fire, like a candle flame. Especially when we're worried or upset," her father went on. "Our imaginations can run away with us. That's probably where all the stories about magic come from. So don't let it bother you," he added in his doctor voice.

His words almost convinced her. It would be easy to believe that she was just upset and sad because she missed Ben. The Hanukkah visions wouldn't be so puzzling if she were making the whole thing up in her mind. But they wouldn't be so interesting, either. At that moment, though, Sarah didn't care whether they were interesting or even true. She wanted to be close to her father, to be a family again, even if it meant agreeing that what she saw wasn't real.

She decided not to say another word about the holiday — but the harder she tried not to think about it, the more it was on her mind. She took another bite of her cinnamon bun, chewed and swallowed, then followed it with a sip of coffee to wash it down.

Then, before she could stop herself, she blurted out, "Dad, how come you don't want to light the Hanukkah candles with Mom and me?"

Her father put down his coffee cup so abruptly that the saucer clattered on the table. Sarah bit her tongue, wishing she could take the words back. Why did I have to go and wreck everything? she thought. Her stomach lurched and she felt sick.

Her father stood up from the table. "I'm sorry, Sarah, I just can't this year. I remember Ben lighting the candles with us and — I just can't." He started clearing the dishes.

"I remember Ben, too," said Sarah. "So does Mom."

"Don't start this, Sarah. I've already talked about this holiday business with your mother. We each have to handle this in our own way, but I certainly don't see anything to celebrate."

This was a different face — not cheerful, but maybe not so angry either. Sad, she thought, and lonely. Maybe they could talk after all. But her father was already leaving the kitchen. "Let's not discuss this again," he said. "Have a good day, Sarah. See you tonight."

His words were ordinary but his voice was like ice, and Sarah felt a chill that she knew wasn't the flu. What if the cross words never went away? What if her dad left, like Raphael's dad? What would happen then?

Now Sarah was desperate to get to school and find out what Raphael had seen in the candles the night before. If he really had seen anything and wasn't just putting her on! She grabbed another cinnamon bun, stuffed it into a sandwich baggie and zipped it into her backpack. She went upstairs to brush her teeth and comb her hair, but saw that the door to Ben's room was open. Usually it was closed and no one went inside. Sarah had gone in once or twice just to look around, but it was too strange; the room still smelled like Ben, even weeks and months after he'd left it.

Now she peeked inside and saw her father sitting on Ben's bed, still covered with its *Star Wars* comforter. He was just sitting there, holding an old transformer toy, turning it over and over in his hands. Sarah thought she saw tears on his cheeks, but she couldn't be sure. She tiptoed down the stairs, got her coat and backpack and slipped out the front door as quietly as she could.

She wanted to talk to Raphael right away but he wasn't at school. Why today? Where could he be? Now she'd have to wait to find out what he'd seen last night, she thought in frustration.

Math was a relief that morning, taking her mind off her thoughts. And when she gave a wrong answer, Mr. Keats said in his encouraging voice, "My friend, that's the best wrong answer I've ever heard." He said that to everyone, but it did make you feel better. "Nobody learns anything without making a mistake" was another one of Mr. Keats' pet sayings. Today he was wearing a black tie with white numbers and plus and minus signs printed on it, like a chalkboard. But Mr. Keats was a good teacher, even with his collection of mottoes and silly ties.

In the last class of the afternoon, they practised for the school Holiday Concert. Sarah's class was singing "Walking in a Winter Wonderland."

On the way home, she took a detour through Kensington Market. Usually she loved to wander around the shops and the racks of clothes crowding the street, looking at all the fashions and odds and ends. But today she felt as if she were seeing double: the way the street looked now and the way it would have looked to Saraleh and her sisters, to Wolf and Anna. It was like being two people at once, with one life in the past and one in the present. She felt special, as if she knew something no one else did.

Sarah stopped in front of one of her favourite stores. She wondered if this old brick house, painted turquoise and blue with pink trim and a fancy pointed roof, might once have been the location of her great-great-grandparents' grocery store. If only she knew the exact address! This shop was called Butterfly and it sold beaded jewellery, sequined belts and fashionable wigs of fake purple hair.

The wigs reminded Sarah of Anna's thick, curly wig. She smiled, remembering how it had flown off Anna's head during her outburst in the kitchen.

Most of the shops had names like Eye of Shiva, Flash-Back, Ego and Astro — names whose meanings Saraleh and her sister Mimi wouldn't even have understood. And the shops sold dresses and skirts at prices that could have fed and clothed their whole family for months. Even Mendel's Cheese Shop — which was probably a relic from the old days — had a sign which read "Cheeses of the World," trying for a modern image.

She fingered vintage lace camisoles, saris from India and GI Joe outfits, but she didn't feel like buying anything today.

Walking along St. Andrew Street toward Spadina Avenue, she passed the Moonbean Café with its tantalizing aroma of fresh-brewed coffee. Then she turned a corner and came face to face with an old brick building, snuggled between a Chinese restaurant and a store that sold hats. She must have passed it a hundred times before without really seeing it, but now she recognized it as a synagogue. She went up the steps and looked at the heavy wooden door. Would it be it open on a Wednesday afternoon? Sarah couldn't read the Hebrew inscription engraved on a plaque over the doorway, but she hoped it meant "Come In."

Above the door, circular stained-glass windows stared down at her like eyes. What did they see?

She tried the door, but it was locked. Sarah felt crushed, without knowing just why. She sank down on the cold stone steps, not sure what to do next, but the air was turning damp and it was getting dark. I'd better get home, she thought, before Mom worries about me. And I've got to find out what happened to Raphael.

Just then, a side door opened and a young man came out, wearing a dark coat and hat. He had the long hair and sidelocks worn by Orthodox Jewish men. As he pulled out a key and locked the door behind him, Sarah stood up.

"Please ..." she said.

He turned his head.

"Could you help me?" she asked.

"Are you lost?"

"No — no, I live nearby. I just wanted to have a look inside."

"We don't have services today. You can come back on Saturday morning with your father and mother," he said in a friendly voice.

"Yes, I guess so," Sarah said, getting up and dusting off her jeans. "But — I'm doing a project for school. I just ... just wanted to have a look inside the building." The lie felt heavy in her mouth, but she didn't know what else to say. She couldn't start telling this stranger about her visions and her feeling that she *had* to look inside this place.

The young man looked at her. "You are Jewish?" he asked.

"Yes. But we don't go to synagogue here. I think my great-great-grandparents used to live in this neighbourhood and own a store, so they might have come to services here. Their names were Wolf and Anna," she added, as if he might recognize them.

"Well, normally we're only open for services, but seeing as I'm here …" He shrugged. "Perhaps I shouldn't do this, but I can let you have a quick look."

The young man took the key from his coat pocket, and unlocked the door. "I am Aaron," he said simply, and Sarah told him her first name, too. Aaron explained that he was doing a degree in Jewish Studies and Architecture at the University of Toronto, and he sometimes helped out at the synagogue.

As he led Sarah through a dark hallway into a gloomy central room with a domed ceiling, he told her that this synagogue had been built by immigrants from a town in Russia, who wanted to create a place of worship like the one they had left back home. He pushed a switch on the wall, and the room glowed with murky light. Sarah's first impression was that she had seen this place before — but when? Behind a central wooden platform stood the Ark, its white curtain shimmering with coloured glass beads and embroidered with gold thread. The dome above was painted with golden stars against a deep blue sky. On the wall behind the Ark were paintings of a lion and a deer, like creatures out of her old Grimm's fairy-tale book, and painted below them were musical instruments, including a drum and a small harp. Rows of benches surrounded the central platform, and upstairs were more benches. Aaron explained these were for the women. "Not like modern synagogues, is it?" he smiled.

And then Sarah knew what was so strangely familiar: this was just like the synagogue from the second night of Hanukkah, when the rabbi talked about seeing miracles. Again Sarah felt that sense of seeing — and *being* — double, as if two worlds were clashing together and she was caught in the middle. Suddenly she wanted to go home, to sit in her own living room with her menorah and see where tonight's candlelight would take her.

"It's getting close to dinnertime," she said to Aaron. "Thanks so much for letting me have a look around. But I have to get home for Hanukkah."

"Yes, I understand. You and your family are welcome to come here on Saturday mornings for services," he said, turning out the lights and leading the way outside. He locked the side door and they walked down the steps together. She watched Aaron vanish into the crowded streets of Kensington Market, his dark clothes barely visible in the dusk. Then Sarah headed for a shortcut to her house.

When she got home, nobody else was there. She decided to check her e-mail before lighting the candles. She didn't have MSN, like Marnie did, and this week she hadn't really thought about e-mail at all, but maybe there was a message from Raphael.

There was — just a short one. "Sorry I wasn't in school today, Sarah. My dad had to go on a day trip to Buffalo for his work, and took me with him. We can talk tomorrow." He ended with one of those happy face smiles. It was good to hear from him, but she was disappointed that his message was so brief. She had so many questions and it was hard to wait.

When she heard someone come in the front door, she went downstairs. It was her mom.

"Your dad's gone to the hospital to see a patient, so he won't be home for a while."

Sarah was a little relieved because she wasn't sure what she'd say to her dad after their talk this morning. "Let's light the menorah," she said to her mom, and they went into the living room. After they lit the candles, her mother sat down at the piano and lifted her hands to the keys.

The music sounded sparkly, like the bright candles. There were six tonight, all blue and white like a summer sky, their light strong and warm. The *Shamas* began to melt from the heat of the candles below. As she listened to the music, Sarah wasn't sure she wanted to go anywhere tonight. For a moment she even had the wild idea of blowing out the candles. But it was too late: it had already started.

She was outdoors, in a light open place. It looked like a big park with rolling hills, flowers in bloom and green, leafy trees. The air was warm — it felt like late spring or summertime. Sarah walked aimlessly, enjoying the scenery, until she noticed something else just ahead: gravestones. Rows of graves. As she came close, she saw both Hebrew and English writing on the stones. So this park was really a cemetery, although it didn't feel dark or gloomy. She shivered, remembering the cemetery where Ben had been buried last summer. That place had given her the creeps, but now, however, she did not feel scared at all. She noticed that most of the graves were very old, and many had pebbles or small stones placed on them. At Ben's funeral, Grandpa A had told her that Jewish people often used stones instead of flowers to remember the dead, because stones were harder and more lasting. "Like memories," he'd added. And they were easier to find, especially in winter or in cities and desolate places.

The stones reminded her of the pebbles Hansel and Gretel used to make a trail and find their way home in the fairy tale — but Ben, like all the people buried here, would never come home again. She figured people might just as well put out bread crumbs for the birds to eat, instead of stones; at least the birds would be happy. Nonetheless, she picked up a smooth white pebble; it fit neatly into the palm of her hand.

As she walked along, Sarah heard birds singing and the sun warmed her skin. She came to an open grassy space encircled by several wooden benches, and noticed a woman resting there, holding a package. When she ventured closer, she saw that the woman was Anna and the package was a baby. Anna patted the empty space next to her on the bench and said, "All alone? You look tired, little one. Come, rest yourself a little, I won't bite."

Sarah sat down. Anna looked happier than when she'd seen her in the kitchen, but there were shadows under her blue eyes. And clearly, Anna didn't remember seeing her before.

The baby stirred. "Her name is Ruth. *Maydela,* a little girl," Anna said, pulling back the blanket covering the baby's face. Anna touched a finger to the baby's mouth, and Ruth made a little kissing sound. She extended her left arm along the top of the bench, and Sarah snuggled against it. Anna held the baby securely with her other arm and began singing a lullaby. It was like the lullaby that Wolf had played on the ship, but Anna had changed the words to fit her new baby:

Raisins and almonds, my little Ruth,
The whole world is open to you,
Everything sweet and strong.
Wherever you go, whatever you do,
Don't forget your mother's song.
Now sleep, little Ruth, sleep

Then she began a new melody:

Zolstu zayn clor,
Mit gezundt un hob a sakh glik
Meyn kind, meyn kind, ah meyn kind

"May your heart be clear," she wished, "and have good health and good luck, my child, my child, my child." They sat in silence as Sarah thought about the words of the song.

"You go to school?" asked Anna, breaking into her thoughts.

"Yes, of course ..." said Sarah. "I mean — yes. My parents think it's important."

"Good, good," said Anna. "Your parents are right. I have three daughters now, and here in this new world, women can be doctors or teachers, write books. As long as they grow up healthy, please God. *Keneinahora* — may the evil eye not see us." A gust of wind blew through the trees and over their faces, ruffling the flowered scarf tied over Anna's head so Sarah could see her thick greyish-blonde curls. "See," said Anna, smiling shyly, lifting one corner of the scarf. "No *sheitel,* no wig. We're in a new country now."

Anna brushed her fingers over the baby's wispy, dark hair. "My parents, my brothers and sisters back in Europe, they don't understand about this country. My husband Wolf and I tell them to come here, we'll help them get started, but they say no. Too hard to leave home, even if things are bad." She looked sad. "I know. I miss home, too. But we had to come here to make a better life. I tell my girls stories so they will know about their grandparents. Fresh milk from the cows, mushrooms from the woods, wine my father used to make. My grandmother's lullabies. Ahhh, so many things to remember."

The baby woke and reached for her mother's face with a little cooing noise. "Here, you want to hold her?" asked Anna.

Sarah was a little nervous but she took the baby, wrapped in her white knitted blanket, and smiled down at her —

at Ruth. She looked about three or four months old and smelled like warm milk. "I'm sure she'll grow up and have a long life," Sarah said. "She'll have a good family. Maybe she'll even do something special, like play the piano."

Anna touched the centre of Sarah's forehead with her finger. "Ahh, my child, you have a gift, I think, a gift of seeing, seeing far. Like the things I see in my dreams. It is not easy having this gift, sometimes you want to give it back. You see things that are not written down in books."

Wolf had said she had healing hands, now Anna thought she had some kind of super-intuition, like ESP. Sarah couldn't tell Anna how she knew what she knew, but she liked the way Anna thought about things. "A gift," she called it. She didn't say it was crazy or weird.

Maybe, she thought, it was because of this special gift that she could see things in the menorah, even though she was not seeing into the future but into the past. Maybe Anna was right, in a way.

The baby reached out a small hand, soft as a flower petal, and grasped Sarah's finger. She remembered how Ben used to do that when he was little. Unable to stop herself, Sarah started to cry. Gently, Anna took the baby, wrapped her more tightly in the wool blanket, and laid her down on the grass. Then she held Sarah close against her broad, firm chest. "*Sha, sha, maydela*, cry, cry. *Zisseh-maydela*," she whispered. "Sweet girl, like sugar."

Sarah cried in great heaving sobs. Her nose ran and her eyes were red, and Anna's white cotton blouse was soaked. "Oh, I'm so sorry," she said in embarrassment.

"So, it will dry," Anna said. "Crying is good for the heart. When babies come into the world, they already know how to cry — and even big girls like you need to remember sometimes. Otherwise you get sick, the tears turn to pickle juice inside you." She gave her a playful tickle in the ribs.

That made Sarah laugh out loud, as hard as she had been crying. Even when the bursts of laughter subsided, she giggled again each time she imagined how it would feel to be full of sour green pickle juice.

"So that's better, all cried out, now you can laugh," said Anna. Then the baby Ruth began wailing noisily. "Now those tears are because she is hungry," said Anna. "That we can do something about." She unbuttoned her blouse, gathered her blue shawl around her shoulders and then picked up Ruth and held the baby to her breast. Sarah watched as Ruth drank hungrily, then gurgled and burped with a little smile on her rosy face. "My little son David is buried here," Anna said softly. "We came to visit him today. But I'm glad I found you. Maybe you were coming to see someone, too?"

"Yes, I … I guess I was. I'm glad you were here." Sarah snuggled up to Anna again. She felt empty but full at the same time. She hadn't cried like that for ages.

It was starting to get cloudy, as if someone had drawn a lace curtain over the sunlight. A few birds were still chirping. "Time to go home," said Anna, rising heavily to her feet.

Sarah hugged her one more time, and gave Ruth a kiss on her soft cheek. "See you again," she said, as Anna hurried off. But will I ever see her again? she wondered. The birdsong started to fade.

The last two candles were flickering out, their flames flaring up one last time. Sarah's mother was playing the final chords of a melody that sounded like clear water running over rocks. Sarah took a deep breath and looked for a tissue to blow her nose. Her eyes were dry, but she felt as if she'd had a good cry. Remembering Anna's gesture, she touched the centre of her forehead. Maybe it is a gift, she thought.

Her mother got up from the piano and sat next to her on the couch. "That felt terrific," she said. "I haven't played like that for ages. I must be terribly rusty."

"No, Mom," said Sarah. "It was great. It really was."

Her mother went to heat up some soup while Sarah went upstairs to finish her homework. She lay on her bed for a while, holding Zachary and thinking of Great-Grandma Ruth as a tiny baby. She was glad that she and Anna had had a chance to spend time together.

Seventh Day:

At school the next morning, Sarah's class was presenting book reports. Mr. Keats had given them a list of books about kids their own age. Sarah's presentation wasn't until the following week, and she was still deep into her novel, the one about a Native mask and a girl and boy who discover its deep power. The mask was carved from a living tree, and Sarah wondered if it had the same kind of magic as her menorah.

Marnie had chosen *The Diary of A Young Girl*, by Anne Frank; she told Sarah it was one of the most amazing books she'd ever read. Anne Frank had written her diary while she and her family and a few friends, all Jews, were hiding from the Nazis in Amsterdam during World War II. The Franks had already moved from Germany to the Netherlands, where they hoped they'd be safe from the concentration camps. But after the Nazis invaded Holland, Jews were in danger there, too.

The family and their friends lived for more than two years in an attic called the "secret annex" over Mr. Frank's office and store, which was now run by the staff who were not Jewish. Only a few trusted employees were in on the secret, and they risked their own lives smuggling in food and supplies, and keeping watch. The attic had more than one room, but even so, stuck in there for so long together, they began to get on each other's nerves. Every minute they were terrified of being discovered.

Marnie was horrified by Anne Frank's story. When she gave her report, she talked excitedly and gestured with her hands. "Slow down," Mr. Keats kept saying. "Some of us haven't read the book — or at least, in my case, not for a long time."

"Did you know that Anne Frank and her family could never go outside when they were hiding in that attic?" Marnie had asked Sarah earlier that morning, as they walked to school together. "It was really crowded and uncomfortable, and she fought with her mom a lot. Imagine never being able to go off by yourself — and being scared *all* the time. But at least she had a boyfriend. And a cat."

"I don't think he was like a real boyfriend," Sarah said. "Not in a place like that." She'd read the book herself, about a year ago, and it still haunted her.

"Sarah!" Marnie had said, with a shocked expression on her face, "I just thought of something! Your family is Jewish. If they hadn't come to Canada when they did, it could have been your Grandma B in that attic! It could have been them."

Sarah nodded. She knew Marnie was right. And now, after her experiences with the Hanukkah candles, she understood better than ever that her relatives had been real people. Now she could picture them in her mind: Wolf and Anna, Saraleh, Mimi, little David and their baby sister Ruth, her own great-grandmother. If Ruth had been killed, she — Sarah — wouldn't even exist, and neither would her mom or Grandma B.

She didn't know much about her father's family. They had come from Europe too, only a few years before World War II. Her dad's grandfather had studied to become a doctor in Vienna, Austria, but he hadn't been allowed to practice medicine in Canada. He didn't have the money to go back to school to get a Canadian degree, so he worked as a pharmacist's assistant and eventually opened his own drugstore in Montreal. His son, her father's father, had worked in the drugstore, too, and later took over the business. Her father had told her that he'd decided to become a doctor because of his grandfather's stories. "My grandfather would have been a really good doctor — he cared about helping people. Of course, they didn't have all the medicines and technology we have now ..." Sarah thought that her father's family must have been brave, as well as lucky, to leave Europe when they did.

"They had to be quiet all day," Marnie told the class now, as she presented her report. Some kids laughed, knowing how hard that would have been for Marnie herself. "They couldn't even flush the toilet before the store closed in the evening!" More laughter, a bit nervous this time, until Mr. Keats raised his hand for silence.

"And then," said Marnie dramatically, "they were captured anyway. They were all killed, except for Mr. Frank, Anne's father. So what was the point of all those years of hiding and worrying? And how could Anne say she still believed, in spite of everything, that people are truly good at heart?"

"At least they tried," Sarah spoke up from her seat. "They hoped they had a chance to stay alive. They didn't just give up."

"Maybe," Marnie agreed, still sounding doubtful.

Marnie finished her report by showing the class some photographs of Anne Frank, her family and their hiding place. "I always thought I was a brave person," said Marnie, "but I don't think I could have done what they did. Trapped inside with so many people and so little to eat. And they didn't even have TV or computers."

"They couldn't have used those things, at least not during the day, even if they had them," Raphael commented. "You said they couldn't even play the radio in daytime because someone might hear it and report them to the Nazis."

"There were a lot of things they didn't have," Mr. Keats pointed out. "Fresh food whenever they wanted it. Fresh air. Exercise. Freedom from fear and freedom to follow their beliefs. Think how lucky we are to live here and now in Canada."

When it was time for questions, talk shifted away from World War II to modern times. Raphael said that September 11, 2001, was one of the scariest world events in their own lives. "So we're not really free from fear, are we?" he asked.

Other kids chimed in, talking about the acts of terrorism and violence reported on the news everyday: suicide bombings, massacres, natural disasters like *tsunamis*.

A soft-voiced girl named Connie pointed out there were kids kidnapped and murdered even right here in Toronto.

The class grew silent as they remembered posters of missing children … their smiling, faded faces.

Mr. Keats tried to get the class's attention back to their book reports, but then gave up. "Well, we might as well call this a current events lesson," he announced.

They were still deep in discussion when the bell rang for lunch. After lunch, Raphael caught up with Sarah as she was leaving the classroom with Marnie. "Let's ask Mr. Keats if we can stay in again and use the computers," he said. "I've got a lot to tell you."

Marnie raised her eyebrows, but Sarah shrugged. "He's just helping me with a science project," she explained. It was pretty close to the truth.

But as they sat in front of the computer, neither of them spoke. Raphael seemed nervous, and Sarah felt strange asking him about his experience. Do I really want to know? she wondered. Finally Raphael said, "I talked to my dad about time travel and stuff when we drove to Buffalo."

"You talked to your dad?!" Sarah didn't want any more people involved. Why didn't Raphael just put it on the internet for everyone to look at?

"Not about what you've been seeing; just general stuff. He said no one knows for sure, but there's a lot more going on in space and time than we think we know. He didn't say time travel was impossible. And he said maybe time isn't like a chart going forward and backward in a straight line. Maybe it's more like the ocean, with lots of waves swirling around making different patterns."

Sarah wrinkled her eyebrows, trying to understand. "I

don't get that," she said.

"Neither do I," Raphael admitted. "At least, not all of it. But it's interesting. And then I started asking my dad about my grandfather. That's what I really want to tell you — how looking at your candles made me remember him. I only met him once or twice, and my dad's never told me much about him. Dad likes to talk, but not usually about family stuff."

Sarah nodded.

"So I was glad we had to go Buffalo," Raphael went on. "It's easier to talk in the car. That's why I like driving with my dad. And with my mom, too." His voice trailed off, and he looked uncomfortable as he began doodling with pencil crayons on a piece of paper. Sarah wondered what he was trying so hard not to say.

"Oh, by the way," Raphael added, "my mom says you can come over on Christmas Eve if you want — we always have a party, with games and food, lots of people. If your parents say it's okay. They're invited, too."

"Sounds good," Sarah said. "Tell your mom thanks. But quit changing the subject; you were going to tell me about what happened the other night."

"Man, that was something," Raphael replied, taking a deep breath. "I saw … something I hadn't thought about for years. Something I didn't even know I knew." He was quiet for a few moments, adding some lines to his drawing.

"Have you ever seen the Northern Lights, Sarah?" he said at last, showing her the picture. It looked like streaks of brilliance in a dark night sky.

"No, I don't think so. What an amazing drawing. You're

really good."

"It's hard to draw them right. You'd remember if you'd ever seen them — they look like alien lights blazing in the sky, and they're incredibly beautiful. My dad and I sometimes see them when we go camping in Algonquin Park. The other night when I looked into the candles, I saw the Northern Lights in all these colours, green and pink and a kind of milky white. I think I was reliving a real memory. My grandfather was there with me, my dad's father. He used to live way up in Northern Ontario. My dad took me there for a week when I was really little.

"I remembered — no, it was like being there — I *felt* my grandfather waking me up really late at night and carrying me outside to look at the sky. He held me way up high, and I thought I could reach out and touch those colours. They were so bright, brighter than the stars or the moon. He touched the top of my head and said, 'Keep this in your mind, boy. Now you've seen the Northern Lights and they're part of you. Part of who you are.' And get this, he whistled at them." Raphael gave a long, low, piercing whistle. "He said that would bring them closer. He said a friend of his who was Cree told him that. I think my grandfather was part Cree too." Raphael whistled again, softer this time.

"We stayed outside all that night," he continued. "My dad was there, too. It was cold, but they wrapped me up in a quilt. And in the morning, just as it was getting light, a deer came out of the woods behind the house and ate some corn out of my grandfather's hand. She let me touch her nose. It was soft, like velvet." He turned to Sarah, his eyes shining. "Maybe that's why I've always liked deer so much. Like that time last year on the scavenger hunt," he said with a shy smile.

"I remember that day," she said. "It was okay. It was nice." Nice seemed a silly word — it didn't say what she meant, but she couldn't think of anything else. "It was really nice."

"I don't know why my grandfather lived up there all alone. My dad said he was studying life. He was going to write a book someday, with stories about his adventures and photographs he took. But he died before he could do it."

"Do you have any of his photographs?" Sarah asked.

Raphael looked thoughtful. "I don't know. I'll ask my dad. I remember him going up there and cleaning out my grandfather's house after he died. It just had one big room and a little alcove for the kitchen. No bathroom even, just an outhouse outside. When my dad came home, he put all the stuff in a big box in the attic."

"Maybe there's pictures of deer or the Northern Lights," Sarah said. "I'd like to see them if you find any."

"I'm going to check, for sure. I remember my dad was in a really bad mood when he came back with the stuff, and I didn't want to ask him about it. I was only about five then. And later, when he moved out, he took the box with him. But I'll ask him next time I go over to his house. Maybe you can come with me sometime."

Raphael picked up a brown pencil crayon and started drawing a deer underneath the Northern Lights. It was so lifelike Sarah thought it would leap off the page.

"You know," Raphael told her, "it was amazing the way

that deer came up to him. It wasn't afraid of him at all."

Raphael sketched some trees around the deer. "My grandfather said something else, too." Raphael hesitated.

"What?" Sarah prompted.

"Well, it might make you feel bad. About your brother."

"What could your grandfather say about Ben?" Her throat tightened up.

"It wasn't about him exactly. Not personally. He said that some Native people believe the Northern Lights are spirits of children who die, or maybe a bridge of light taking them to another world."

Sarah felt her eyes prickle with tears and she wiped them with the back of her hand. She didn't want Raphael to see her cry, but it was such a beautiful idea. She could almost see Ben shining up there in living colour. He would have liked crossing that bridge. He always loved driving over bridges on car trips — the changing rhythm and noise of the wheels, the dizzying view of the water, the steel structures towering like giant Lego. Sometimes when they drove over the Burlington Skyway, he'd imagine they were going up to the sky. Well, maybe now he's up there, seeing the Northern Lights glow like giant traffic lights, she thought.

"Sarah?…"

"I think Ben would have liked that idea. He didn't want to be buried in the earth." Ben had told her that, right near the end. She'd never said anything to her parents. They'd gotten so busy making arrangements for the funeral and burial that she didn't want to cause any extra trouble.

"Your menorah is so awesome," Raphael said. "I wonder

how it works — how it makes us see things. But hey, Sarah, tell me more about what you've seen. Is it like what happened with me?"

"Not exactly," Sarah answered. "I go further back into the past and see people I've never actually met in my life, except for one little girl who I think is my great-grandmother. It has something to do with a boy, I think he was my great-uncle or something, who died a long time ago. He reminds me of Ben. And he had a sister named Sarah.

"And another thing that's really weird," she added, "is that I can understand what they're saying, even though they don't speak English. It's amazing seeing these people, Raphael. I feel so close to them — sometimes even more than my parents. But why do you think all this is happening now?"

Raphael thought a moment. "You tell me, Sarah."

"Because of the menorah? Because it came from Russia and belonged to all those people in the past ... and now we're using it for the first time?" Sarah wasn't quite sure that was the whole reason. Would Raphael understand if she told him that it was a miracle, like the one in the Hanukkah story? Or would he want some scientific explanation? Maybe "miracle" wasn't the whole answer, either.

"Well, the menorah, of course," said Raphael. "And ... and I think it's about Ben, too. You all miss him. What if this is his way of sticking around for a while or sending you messages?"

"That could be it," Sarah answered, choosing her words carefully. "But I think it's these relatives from the past, not

Ben, who want to get in touch with me."

"I see what you mean," said Raphael. "Maybe they want to know you, and they're using the menorah to do it."

"Yes, and I'm glad to know them. But why now? And what *do* they want to tell me? Wait," she said excitedly. "I've just figured something out! I think they want to help me deal with Ben's death ... that's a big part of why this is happening. And the menorah is what connects us." More and more pieces of the puzzle began to click into place in her mind, fitting together just right. She fell silent, thinking.

"What?" asked Raphael after a moment, as if she'd said something out loud.

"Nothing. I was just thinking."

After another pause, Raphael said, "I've just thought of something, too. Why would I see *my* grandfather, with *your* menorah?"

This was a new question, and a hard one. "I don't know — maybe it works for anyone, at the right time," Sarah mused. "Maybe it's because he wants to help you deal with your parents and everything."

Just then, the bell rang to begin afternoon classes. Raphael offered Sarah his drawing, but she told him to keep it and show it to his dad. Mr. Keats came into the room and asked them to take their seats. Today he was wearing a tie with a pattern of reindeer and sleighs. The red noses of the reindeer were so bright they almost glowed.

That night when Sarah lined up the multicoloured candles — seven, only one space left empty — she remembered the

Northern Lights and hoped she would see them someday. She wondered if you could see them in the city; there were so many street lights and neon signs in Toronto, sometimes you could hardly see the stars. But it was comforting to think that Ben could be out there somewhere.

Then she thought of Anne Frank, shut away in her attic for over two years, never going outside to see the sky at all, day or night. She agreed with Marnie — she didn't think she could live like that, either. But maybe you never knew what you would do until it happened. She didn't let her thoughts get to what happened after they were discovered and sent to the concentration camp.

Sarah was alone in the house after the candles were lit, but she didn't mind. She and her mother had lit the candles together in the living room, and tonight her father had actually watched from the doorway. Then her parents had gone out to dinner and a movie. They'd looked more relaxed, going out like that. Her mother had wanted to call the high school student who used to babysit for Sarah and Ben, but Sarah said no, she'd be all right, she'd be fine. She was twelve, old enough to be left alone for the evening. She'd do her homework and she'd call Marnie if anything came up; Marnie's mother was always home. And she'd go to sleep at a reasonable time. Yes, she loved them too. Goodbye.

Flames swirled up, then faded and disappeared. She saw the menorah — her menorah — standing on a windowsill. It looked a little more worn than the time before, but it was still shiny. It held seven candles waiting to be lit. This time Sarah was not in the store or the rooms behind it, nor in the apartment where the girls played *dreidel* and ate *rugelah*. This was another place entirely, a kitchen, larger and better furnished than the one before. There was a new girl, a little younger than she was, maybe nine or ten, sitting on a chair at the kitchen table and writing on thin blue paper. She was wearing a cotton dress that came to her knees and a wool cardigan. A calendar on the wall read "December 1938," and showed a picture of snow-covered trees.

Sarah heard footsteps. A woman came hurrying into the kitchen to stir a soup bubbling in a large iron pot on the stove. She could smell tomatoes, onions, garlic and other vegetables — delicious! This stove was more modern than the one in Anna's kitchen. Sarah saw flames under the pot and realized it was a gas stove, like their one at home. There were electric lights on the ceiling and appliances, though they looked old-fashioned — a refrigerator with rounded corners, a shiny metal toaster, an iron. Time had moved on. And they were speaking English.

"Look, Mama," said the little girl, "I'm writing to Pavel and Eva, to wish them a happy Hanukkah."

"A happy Hanukkah," echoed the woman. "It will be a miracle if your cousins can even celebrate Hanukkah — that will be the miracle!"

"Why, Mama? Why can't they? Is something the matter?"

"*Sha, sha,* never mind, Beatrice. You are too young for your head to be filled with trouble and *tsouris*. Just write to them, I'm sure they'll be happy to hear from you. Draw them a picture, you're good at drawing."

Sarah stared at the little girl. Beatrice. Bea. Could this be Grandma B?

Then her Mama would be …

"Ruth, I'm here with the *latkes*," called out a firm, friendly voice as another woman bustled into the kitchen, carrying a plate wrapped with a white cloth napkin. "Let's put them in the oven to keep warm."

"Thank you, Sarah. You make the best *latkes*. Of the three of us, you got Mama's gift for cooking. Probably because you were her favourite kitchen helper."

"Sure! More probably it's because I love to eat!" She patted her hips. "Also, I was the oldest. By the time you came along, Mama didn't want to train a new helper," she joked.

These women must be Saraleh and Ruth, now grown up. Saraleh still had red hair, although it was shorter now and streaked with grey. As she'd said, she was certainly not thin; her body curved and bulged pleasantly, like angel food cake.

"Look, Tante Sarah, I'm writing to my cousins in Prague. I've drawn them a picture of the menorah and of our house," said Beatrice, getting up to show the picture to her aunt.

"You should be writing to their parents again, Ruth, or at least Morris should. They're his relatives after all. Why won't they listen? They should come over to Canada now, while there's still time. Hitler's already moving into Czechoslovakia; Germany's not big enough for him."

Ruth wiped her hands on her flowered apron and poured boiling water from a kettle into a bright red teapot. She was thinner than her sister and had the same bird-like quickness that Sarah had noticed when Ruth was a little girl playing with the *dreidel* — and that she still had, now Sarah thought of it, even as an old, old lady.

"We write, we write," she said. "Morris writes all the time. He sends money, even. Not that we can afford it, but what else can we do? They write back and say it might not be so bad if they stay in Prague."

"What are they waiting for — the Messiah to come?"

"Hush, Sarah! Don't talk like that. It's not respectful," warned Ruth.

"I'm sorry. It's just that the news has me so upset. Ruthie, you read about what happened in Germany last month! They're calling it Crystal Night, *Kristallnacht* — the night of the broken glass."

"Please, Sarah, the *maydela*. The little one."

"So she'll hear and she'll know it's not easy to be a Jew, especially not now, not in Europe. Such a night of hatred! Broken glass everywhere — shop windows, even synagogues. Blood, broken bodies. People hurt for just minding their own business. And they have to wear the Star of David sewn on to their clothes, too, so everyone will know they are Jews. It's like the pogroms all over again."

"And remember the big riot at Christie Pits, right here in Toronto a few years ago," said Ruth, shaking her head at the memory. "Mobs — even here! I hate to think of it — young Canadian men carrying swastika banners and fighting with young Jewish men. And right near our old neighbourhood. At a baseball game, of all places." She ran her hands through her dark hair. "What were they thinking? As if we're not good Canadians, too. But at least we stood up for ourselves."

"We need to fight back sometimes, like the Maccabees," agreed Tante Sarah.

"But why can't people just get along?" asked Ruth. "We're all human beings."

"Unless we're aliens from outer space," piped up Beatrice.

"What did you say?" Ruth asked in a sharp voice.

"We're all human beings unless we're aliens from outer space," Beatrice repeated. A mischievous little smile played on the girl's face.

"Aliens from space! *Feh!* Such creatures don't even exist, thank God," said Tante Sarah. "Otherwise they might fly down from the sky and eat you up," she said, winking at Beatrice to show she was teasing.

"Beatrice, you've been listening to the radio too much," Ruth told her. "She's thinking about that *War of the Worlds* story that frightened everyone a couple of months ago," she said to her sister. "Imagine making up stories like that, especially the way things are now, with maybe a real war of the worlds coming again!" She turned back to Beatrice. "Listen to me: that was all made up, not true at all." Ruth gave the soup several energetic stirs, as if she were lecturing it, too.

"Well, enough politics. I made applesauce," said Tante

Sarah, opening a glass jar. "You know, I wish Mimi were here, so we'd be all together for Hanukkah the way we used to be, bless Mama and Papa's memory. Why did she ever go down to New York?"

"She was lucky to get that job as a newspaper writer. She always wanted to be different," Ruth said, "and to make a name for herself."

"Well, she'll have a lot to write about with what's going on in Europe. Let's hope the world comes to its senses soon." She put her arm around her sister's shoulders. "Maybe she'll remember to send us a clipping of one of her stories."

Ruth gave her sister a kiss on the cheek. "I'm so glad you're here, Sarah, especially with Morris away on his business trip. Here, let's have a cup of tea while it's still hot. Then we'll light the candles before dinner." She poured them each a cup, and the two women sat down at the table with Beatrice.

Sarah wanted to burst into the conversation and tell them about Anne Frank and the Nazis and everything she knew would happen soon. This was 1938; in only one year World War II would start, and it would last six long years. She wished so much she could tell them — maybe they could try harder to persuade their cousins in Prague to leave.

But this time, like the earlier night when the three girls played *dreidel*, she couldn't get them to see or hear her. It was as if she were enclosed in some kind of force field.

Of course, she thought: it's because Grandma B and Ruth were still alive in her own time. But then she remembered seeing Ruth with her mother in the cemetery, when Anna made Sarah laugh by telling her about the pickle juice. She thought harder: Ruth had been a tiny baby then, unable to speak or even have clear memories. Maybe that didn't count; the "invisibility rule" only applied when people were old enough to talk and remember.

Being invisible had some advantages, as Sarah could move around without having to explain herself. She peered over Beatrice's shoulder as she wrote her letter. This little-girl Beatrice had the same intense dark eyes as Grandma B had now, and she had dark brown bangs that tumbled over her forehead as she leaned forward, intent on her work.

On the table in front of her, Beatrice had a heart-shaped candy box, and when she had finished her letter, she opened it and carefully took out a folded piece of paper. "Here's the drawing of the yellow butterfly Eva sent me in her last letter," she said. She unfolded the paper and showed them a picture of a yellow butterfly with feathery green antennae and blue dots like eyes on the wings. "Look, Mama, how beautiful it is! I'm going to put it up on my wall." In the corner of the picture was a little face, with some words in a comic strip balloon. "Pavel wrote something here, but I can't read it."

Her Aunt Sarah looked at the paper. "It says: '*Fly away, butterfly, up to the dazzling sun, yellow as you are.*' Such a modern girl, she can't read Yiddish," she said, gently pinching the little girl's cheek. She looked at the paper again, and smiled. "Very nice. They are artists and poets, your cousins. Listen, Ruth, I'll give you some more money for them. I'm earning a good salary now, and I have no family to support.

We'll ask Mimi for something, too. We'll find a way ..."

"Yes," said Ruth. "I'll just have to wait a little longer for my piano. No matter." She hugged her daughter and told her, "Yes, my sweetheart, put that butterfly on the wall. It will brighten up this dark time. Like the Hanukkah candles. Come, let's light them together." The two women and the little girl said the traditional prayer and lit the candles. Sarah watched them, filled with longing to be part of their group, but her heart felt peaceful and calm. *"Baruch atoi Adonai ... "* she whispered along with them.

Sarah had never heard of these relatives in Czechoslovakia. She wondered if they had been able to get to Canada safely. Who could tell her about them? Ruth was so old herself now, and her husband Morris had died a long time ago, years before Sarah was born. Saraleh and Mimi were dead, too. She wished she could have met them just once, for real, and asked them about their lives. Christie Pits, for instance — that was the same place, not far from her house, where she and her friends often went tobogganing down the steep hills and where people still played baseball in the summer. Did people really have a riot there? Maybe her mother or father would know, or her grandparents. And what about Mimi? Did she become a reporter in New York? What kind of stories did she write?

Beatrice laid the drawing of the butterfly flat against the wooden kitchen table and carefully smoothed out the creases. The picture glowed as if the crayons themselves had been made of light. It looked familiar, thought Sarah. Where had she seen it before?

Ruth and her sister had set the table and served the food, and now the family sat down to eat their soup and *latkes*. The savoury smells made Sarah hungry, and she could almost hear her stomach growling. The candles flickered cheerfully on the windowsill, lighting up the paper butterfly, making it seem to fly away into the sunlight. Sarah followed it with her eyes as long as she could, until she felt herself fluttering and whirling in space.

Sarah rubbed her eyes. She was home again, curled up on the couch in a cocoon of blankets and cushions. The candles were almost burnt out; just one tiny flame remained. She got up and stretched, then wandered into the kitchen to get a glass of milk. She decided to make herself a piece of toast with peanut butter and honey. Even though she'd had a couple of slices of pizza before her parents went out, she was famished again. While waiting for her toast to pop up, she looked at the kitchen bulletin board. This year her mother had bought a calendar showing children's drawings from all over the world. The picture for December was a polar bear drawn by a boy from Nunavut. Sarah took the calendar off its hook and flipped through the pages. There it was, the picture for June — a bright yellow butterfly with blue and green markings. "Terezin concentration camp, Czechoslovakia, 1942," the caption read. "Artist unknown." The picture shone like the sun. Underneath were a few lines from a poem, whose author was also unknown:

Such, such a yellow
Is carried lightly 'way up high
It went away I'm sure because it wished to
kiss the world goodbye.

The words "concentration camp" gave her a prickle of fear. Terezin was in Czechoslovakia. Could this be another picture and poem by Beatrice's cousins? Would that mean they hadn't escaped to Canada, after all?

So much had happened this week and she had found out things about her family that she could never have imagined, dreamed or made up. After she'd gone upstairs and put on her nightgown, she lay awake thinking of the lost cousins. As she wondered again about the butterfly picture, she drifted off to sleep, with one of those dreams of flying so real it could almost be true.

Eighth Day:

Sarah awoke to a city white and muffled, like a scene on a greeting card. She looked out the window at the falling snow and the soft timeless light before squinting at the clock — 7:45. Oh no, I'll be late, she thought; then she remembered with a wonderful sense of relief that this was a PD day and there was no school. She drifted back to sleep and dreamed of a snowglobe she'd had when she was little, a souvenir from a trip to Northern Ontario on the Polar Bear Express train. When you shook it, a cloud of snowflakes swirled around the miniature houses and trees nestled inside. In the dream, she was inside the globe, too; a tiny person lost in a snowstorm.

When she woke up again, just after nine o'clock, the snow had stopped and the sun was shining. She thought of the night before, when she'd seen Grandma B as a little girl writing to her cousins in Prague. She wondered again what had happened to Pavel and Eva. And Ruth and her sister had talked about Crystal Night — a beautiful name for an ugly thing. Sarah was glad she was living here and now.

She suddenly wanted to get outside, into the bright,

fresh whiteness. She jumped out of bed and got dressed, went downstairs and flung open the front door. The street was transformed into a "Crystal Day." Icicles sparkled on the branches and dripped from the roofs, and the snow glistened under a clear blue sky and dazzling sunlight.

After checking with her mother, Sarah phoned Marnie to ask her to go tobogganing at Christie Pits. Marnie had a sled called a snow-racer and Sarah had a snow-tube, a kind of tire that you inflated and sat on to go whirling down the hill. Marnie's mother drove them to the park around eleven o'clock, and, after warning them to "drive carefully," she went home, saying she'd pick them up in a couple of hours.

Lots of kids were there already, using every kind of sled: new inflatable ones, simple sheets of plastic, long wooden toboggans for three or more people. They were wearing every kind of winter outfit, too, from weatherproof snowmobile suits to hockey sweaters to old coats with bright woollen toques and mittens. There were moms and dads helping little ones, and even some high school kids enjoying the morning off. The place looked so full of happy life that Sarah couldn't imagine people ever fighting there.

Sarah waved to some kids from school; then, as she and Marnie trudged up the hill after their first flight down, Sarah saw Ben's best friend, Jamie. The sight of him jumping and playing in the snow scraped a raw place in her mind. She could remember taking Jamie and Ben tobogganing on a day just like this a couple of winters ago.

Raphael and a couple of his friends, Dave and Jesse,

suddenly appeared out of nowhere, speeding past them on a sleek wooden toboggan. Raphael gave her a big smile on the way by, but he was holding on too tight to wave. They all met up at the top of the hill, the guys horsing around, play fighting. Sarah noticed that Raphael was rougher and noisier than he usually was when he was alone with her.

"Come on, let's race," said Dave.

"There's too many of us," Sarah said. "We could crash."

"No way," said Jesse. "There's tons of room. How about it, Raphael? You up for it?"

"You know it," Raphael answered. "Don't worry, Sarah, we'll be fine. Marnie, you game?"

"Absolutely!" said Marnie.

"Sure, she's cool," added Dave, grinning.

Marnie had confided to Sarah that she really liked Dave.

"Here's how we'll set up the first race," Dave told them. "Sarah, you get into your tire, Marnie'll be on her snow-racer, and Jesse, Raph and I will take the long toboggan. Next time we'll trade toboggans. Come on, we'll show you how fast this thing can go!" Dave was built like a football player, just like his two older brothers, and he liked being in charge.

"In your dreams!" said Marnie.

Jesse, a small, dark-haired boy with a booming voice, called out, "On your mark, get set, GO!" from his position in the front of the toboggan.

Sarah felt butterflies in her stomach for a moment when she took off. Then, speeding downhill through the powdery, sparkling snow, she felt a rush of clear, clean air sweep over her. The wind was so cold it hurt to breathe but it felt wonderful at the same time. She stretched back in the tire, gazing up into bluest sky she had ever seen, with sunshine so bright it was blinding. Hurtling down the steep slope, she felt like an angel — a snow-angel — flying through space and time. Heavy weights seemed to lift from her body, making her lighter than air. Her face was wet with snow and her cheeks tingled. She was glad to be alive, alive and free, on a day like this.

"Beat all of you!" Marnie sang out cheerfully. "Told you so!"

"And we beat you, Sarah," said Dave, grinning.

Sarah didn't care. She had won, too, broken through some barrier as real as sound or light or gravity. She felt she could let go of the sadness and fear that had been weighing her down for so long. Even the visions from the menorah seemed far away. She was flying on her own, entering another dimension.

"What're you smiling about? You came in last," Dave said to her.

But she knew better. She kept smiling, even laughing, as she and her friends marched back up the hill, ready to do it all over again. They took turn after turn, race after race, trading sleds so that Sarah or Marnie, or both of them, rode on the large toboggan while one or two of the boys took the racer and the tire. When Sarah sat behind Raphael on the toboggan, gripping his red parka with her gloved hands, she felt an extra jolt of excitement. "Hang on tight, Sarah," he said. "Off we go, into the Wild Blue Yonder!"

Sarah was sure she could go on like this all day. She could do anything!

Then it happened.

She was on the snow-racer again even though she didn't like it much. As she swerved to avoid a little kid, she struck a patch of ice and skidded wildly toward a pine tree that suddenly loomed up in front of her, taller than tall, stretching into the sky. She tried to stop, steer clear, even jump off, but everything happened so quickly. She felt as if she were inside the glass globe, swallowed up in a raging blizzard. Someone was shaking the glass hard, shaking, shaking, shaking … so much swirling snow that she couldn't see, couldn't hear, couldn't think.

She woke up in a strange bed in a strange room.

For a few seconds she couldn't remember anything, then she saw snow, toboggans, a pine tree hurtling toward her. But that was silly, trees didn't move. She saw Marnie and Raphael looking down at her as she lay on the ground. She couldn't seem to move. Why was Marnie crying? Raphael was squeezing her cold hand, brushing snow off her face …

"Sarah — sweetheart — are you okay? Thank goodness you're back with us." Her father was stroking her cheeks, her hair.

"Back? What happened, Dad?"

"You had a hit-and-run accident with a tree while you were sledding, and you hit your head. The tree is still standing, by the way." He cupped his hand under her chin and gave her a "doctor" look. "You'll be okay too, but good grief, Sarah, you don't do things by halves, do you? Luckily, some boy named Raphael had his dad's cell phone with him, so Marnie called us right away. Sarah, for … Pete's sake, Sarah, why do you take such chances?" His voice got louder, almost angry.

"I don't take chances, Dad," Sarah protested. "I was just sledding. I was — having fun."

He didn't reply but clasped her hand gently.

"Where are we — I mean, what hospital, Dad? And where's Mom?"

"Sick Kids," her father answered, looking at her strangely. "I would have thought you'd recognize it." He looked around the cubicle. "Actually, you're in the emergency room, but I think they want to keep you upstairs overnight. And your mother just went to the washroom — she'll be right back."

Her mother came in as he was talking. Her eyes were red and puffy, and her face was pale.

"Hi, Mom," Sarah said.

Her mother just hugged her and held her tight.

"I haven't been asleep this whole time, have I?" Sarah asked. She was beginning to remember doctors and nurses hovering around her, hands stitching and bandaging, an X-ray machine whirring. She reached up and felt gauze and tape on her forehead, above her left eyebrow.

Her father explained that, according to Marnie, she'd passed out for just a few moments when she hit the tree, but she'd been dozing off and on ever since. "We don't want you to sleep too deeply until we're sure your head is okay. You have a mild concussion and a cut on your forehead, but no bones broken."

Sarah sat up again, feeling more alert. "I'm fine now. Can't I go home?" she asked. "I've just got a little headache." Then the room spun around a couple of times, and she lay back dizzily on the pillow. Suddenly the whole last week came back to her in a flash. "What day is it?" she asked. "What time is it?"

Her father laughed, a warm laugh like the old days. "That's what you always used to ask when you woke up from a nap when you were little," he said. "It's still Friday, Friday the thirteenth. An unlucky day — but lucky too, because you're not hurt too badly. And it's about ..." he checked his watch. "... about three-thirty."

"Good, there's still time. Will they let us have Hanukkah here? Can someone go get the menorah and candles?"

"Well, I don't want to leave you," her mother began. "Besides, I don't know if the hospital would ..."

"Couldn't one of you go? Please. It's the last night — it's really important." She pulled anxiously at the thin white blanket.

Her parents exchanged one of those "what-do-you-think?" looks.

"I'll get them," said her father finally. "It's no problem."

"Wait, Dad, as long as you're going — can you bring my blue nightie, it's on my bed, and my toothbrush, and that novel, it's on the bed, too. The one about the mask."

"I better get going before the list gets too long," her

father smiled, giving her a kiss as he left.

A few minutes later, two orderlies came to move Sarah to her room on the ward. She felt dizzy and sick to her stomach when they shifted her onto the stretcher, but she perked up after she got settled in bed.

She was in a room with three other beds, all empty. Two of the beds were neatly made up, but the third one had a pink bathrobe lying across the foot and a fluffy stuffed elephant on the pillow. The elephant wore a balloon saying "Get Well" tied to its trunk. A nurse bustled around, pointing out the bathroom and showing Sarah how to adjust the bed and use the call button.

"They've taken that little girl for X-rays," the nurse said, waving at the bed with the elephant. "Her name's Amy. She was in a car accident and broke some ribs. But she'll be okay." She handed Sarah a paper cup of lukewarm ginger ale. "A liquid diet for you for today — doctor's orders," she explained. "See you later."

"How do you feel, honey?" her mother asked when they were alone.

"Pretty good. My head still hurts a little, but now I'm starving. And this ginger ale is completely flat. Can't I have some ice cream?"

Her mother went out to ask the nurses. Soon she returned, accompanied by an older nurse with a friendly face who handed Sarah an orange popsicle. Even without looking at her name tag, Sarah recognized her — it was Patricia, the nurse who had told her about leukemia. Sarah reminded her who she was.

"Hi. You took care of my brother Ben — Ben Goldman — when he was here last spring."

"Oh, yes," said Patricia. "I thought I recognized you. We all liked Ben so much, he was such a brave boy."

"We really miss him," Sarah answered.

"Of course you do," she said. "Listen, you go on with your visit, and I'll look in on you later."

After the nurse left, her mother said, "You know, that's the first time I've heard you say you miss Ben."

"Is it?" Sarah was shocked. "I think it all the time." They were both silent. "I guess it's hard to say out loud," she finally added.

"I guess it is," said her mother, stroking Sarah's hair.

They both looked up as the little girl from the other bed came back from X-rays with her mother. The mother smiled sympathetically at Sarah's mom and gave a little wave before she pulled the curtains around Amy's bed. I guess they want some privacy, thought Sarah.

She looked out the window, which was right beside her own bed. It was getting dark, and she could see the thin golden crescent of a new moon rising between two skyscrapers. This was a different ward than the one Ben had stayed in, but all hospital rooms looked and smelled pretty much the same.

Her father returned just as Sarah's dinner of chicken broth and green Jell-O arrived. He'd used Sarah's school backpack to carry her things, and he had also brought sandwiches and coffee for her mother and himself.

"By the way," he said, "there were two phone messages

for you. Marnie wanted to know how you are. She sounded so worried I called her back and told her you're going to be fine. And the other was that boy with the artist's name — Raphael. He said he was really sorry. I believe he said 'really, really.' Was it his idea to go racing, Sarah?"

"No, no, it wasn't his fault at all. Did he say anything else?"

"He said he'll see you soon, and he hopes you light your 'awesome' candles." He looked at the box of candles in his hand. "I never heard Hanukkah candles called 'awesome' before. Still, he sounds like a nice boy."

"I liked him when he came to the house the other day," said her mother. "He seemed very smart. And polite."

Just then, Amy's mother drew back the curtains, gave them another smile and kissed Amy goodbye before leaving. Sarah concentrated on her Jell-O, glad for the interruption.

When the tray was cleared, Sarah set up the candles in the menorah. She chose red, green, yellow, blue, and repeated the pattern; then she picked a white candle for lighting the others. All eight were in place tonight, as well as the *Shamas:* nine altogether. Sarah was glad she could complete the ceremony, even if it had to be here in the hospital.

"You've really kept the holiday going this year," her mother said. She set the menorah on the bedside table, scraping off a few bits of wax from the lion's mane. "This is so beautiful, isn't it? And it brings back lots of memories. I'm glad Grandma Ruth kept it all this time."

"I've checked with the nurse and she says we're fine as long as we don't set off the smoke detector," said Sarah's father.

Amy was watching curiously from her bed, and Sarah's mother gave her a warm smile. "It's part of our holiday celebration," she explained. Amy was about seven or eight, and she looked scared, clutching her stuffed elephant.

"It's okay if you want to leave, Dad," Sarah said.

"Maybe I'll just go outside for a minute ..." he began, turning toward the door. Then he stopped. "No," he said, "I'll stay. I haven't been around much this holiday, and I think — no, I *know* — it's time we started doing things as a family again. I've been thinking about our talk the other morning, Sarah, and today, when you said you just wanted to have fun ... well, that got me thinking even more. Maybe we all need to have some fun, even after ... even if it's hard to get started."

Sarah just nodded.

Her father lightly touched the bandage on her head. "We can be grateful for one miracle, at least — you're okay. You know, sweetheart, your mother and I couldn't bear it if anything happened to you, too."

Sarah's mom held up a pack of matches. "Come on," she said, "it's time to light the candles."

What would she see tonight? And would her parents see anything? She had to prepare them somehow for what might happen. "Mom and Dad — I need to tell you something. This isn't an ordinary menorah."

"What do you mean?" her mother asked.

"Well, all this week I've been seeing things, like dreams but more real, when I light the candles. I tried to tell you about it, Dad," she added.

"Yes, I remember."

"I just wanted to warn you in case you see something, too."

"Well, we're all here together, so let's just light the candles and see what happens," her mother said, looking sideways at Sarah's dad. She struck a match and lit the *Shamas* before handing the white candle to Sarah.

Sarah lit each of the eight candles, one by one, as they said the blessing together and ended with "Happy Hanukkah." From outside the door came the sound of Christmas carols playing on someone's radio.

As the flames steadied, the room was enveloped in a hazy glow. Sarah felt sleepy and peaceful and her headache was gone. She was home in her own bed. Ben was climbing up to her, holding his bear, Zachary, crying after a bad dream. She wanted to push him out and send him to her parents' room but he was so warm and soft in his fuzzy yellow sleepers, almost as furry as the bear, that she let him cuddle up next to her. His breath smelled like apples. She put her arms around him and told him all the stories she could think of to help him get back to sleep: *The Little Engine that Could, Jack and the Beanstalk, Where the Wild Things Are,* even a new book she had just read called *The Snow Cat.* It was like being there again, living it one more time, just like Raphael's visit with his grandfather. Ben alive and loved. She had completely forgotten that night until now.

She lived more and more scenes with Ben from the recent past, her own lifetime. Fights they'd had over Ben wanting to play with her things, and the time he'd pestered her to put all the water she'd just sprinkled on her garden right back into the watering can, so he could pour it into his wading pool — even when she kept telling him that was impossible. And the first day of kindergarten, when he'd told Jamie that he wouldn't cry because his big sister was there in the same building, in Room 202.

She could feel Ben's sturdy body close to hers. Even the grey eyes that had asked "Will I get well?" did not seem so haunting. Nearby, she saw Saraleh, Mimi, Wolf and Anna, and the baby David smiling at her, caring about her. She realized that all these people — even Ben — were ghosts, but not scary, hungry, creepy Halloween-type ghosts. They were simply people from the past whom she was able to meet. She was living a ghost story with a difference.

She gave Ben one last hug under the covers. With a small, watchful part of her mind, she saw her mother and father also looking at the candles, sitting very still. She somehow knew without a doubt that they were each having their own thoughts of Ben and other people they loved from long ago. Then she found herself back in her hospital bed, looking at the menorah, the candles still burning brightly. One by one, they began to flicker and go out. She remembered how Ben used to make the family guess which candle would last the longest.

"I bet that red one," Sarah said now.

"The blue one on the end," said her mother, her eyes moist.

"No, the yellow one near the middle," chimed in her father, coughing a little.

In the end, it was a green one, Ben's favourite colour. It seemed to wink at them before dying.

"That was neat," said Amy from her bed. "I liked watching those candles. They made me think of my Grandma. She just died last year."

Amy, too?

"I'm not sure what just happened here," her father said. "but I'm glad I stayed. What did Raphael say — 'awesome'?"

Sarah's mother took her husband's hand and held it. "This menorah is a gift — a gift to all of us."

They were all holding hands close together when Patricia came in to check on Sarah.

"Sorry to break up your party, but this girl needs her beauty sleep. She's going home tomorrow," she told them firmly. Sarah assured her parents that she felt well enough to stay by herself overnight.

"See you in the morning, sweetie," her parents said, after the nurse left.

"Good night."

"Good night."

Sarah looked out the window once more before she fell asleep. The crescent moon was gone, but she could see a few stars in the deep velvet sky.

Ninth Day:

Sarah woke up to see sunlight filtering into the room through the window blinds. Her headache was all better, but it took her a few minutes to figure out that she was in a hospital bed, and to remember why. Then it all came back — the joy of flying down the hills of snow, feeling anything was possible, feeling lighter than air.

She saw the empty menorah on the night table next to her glass of ginger ale, and she came back to earth with a thud. It wasn't just that she remembered crashing into the tree. She realized that Hanukkah was over. The menorah would be put away on the shelf for another year and the visions would be gone. She had come to count on the menorah and the people she met back in time for comfort, for support, for understanding. She remembered how surprised and scared she'd been at first, and then how she'd looked forward to each visit with excitement and hope. What would she do now?

Seven days of creation, eight days of Hanukkah, but the ninth day was just a big question mark.

Then she remembered the helper candle, the *Shamas*, the

one that did all the work. The ninth candle. Maybe it's up to me now, she thought, slowly climbing out of the high metal bed.

Maybe I can be the helper. But how?

Sharing last night with her parents had been wonderful, but was it enough? Would things really be better at home?

She remembered her talk with the rabbi. After the eighth day, people went back to ordinary life. He wasn't sure that was an important part of the story, but she thought it should be. The rabbi had said that ordinary things could be precious, and even Anne Frank had written about everyday problems like schoolwork and housework, her feelings about her friend Peter, her conflicts with her father, mother and sister. Ordinary life, even in those dangerous times.

And then Sarah realized that the people she'd met had not vanished completely. They had become part of her and they would stay around even after the holiday. Hanukkah didn't have to be over — the ninth day could be a beginning, not an end.

"Hi," said a small voice, and Sarah looked over to Amy's bed, where the little girl was just waking up.

"Hi back at you," Sarah said.

She was sitting up on the bed when a new nurse came to check her temperature and blood pressure and brought over her clothes from the cupboard. The nurse also changed her bandage, neatly taping a smaller one over the cut on Sarah's forehead. Sarah winced when the nurse cleaned the area around the cut. "You'll hardly have a scar," the nurse remarked. "And it'll be covered up by your hair. By the way," she added, "Patricia went off duty at midnight but she said to say goodbye. She left this for you," and she gave Sarah a small candy cane.

"Thanks," Sarah replied, looking at her face in the mirror and wondering about the scar. It'll remind me of this Hanukkah forever, she thought as she got dressed.

Then an orderly brought in her breakfast tray. Real food! She began to eat her oatmeal while she waited for her parents to come take her home.

As she ate, she had an idea. She wondered why she hadn't thought of it before. She could hardly wait to ask her parents.

As soon as her mother and father came to pick her up, Sarah asked "Can we go visit Great-Grandma Ruth in the nursing home? Right now?"

"What's this about?" asked her mother.

"I want to thank her for the menorah, and I just want to see her. Isn't that okay?" Sarah thought that if she could see her great-grandmother now — after seeing her as a baby, a little girl and the young mother of Beatrice — she could connect the dots of everything that had happened and bring the two worlds together. It would be the perfect thing to do on the ninth day. She wished she'd listened more carefully to Ruth's stories on past visits; she'd certainly pay attention this time!

"Of course it's okay," said her mother. "As a matter of fact, Grandma Ruth invited us to a holiday lunch at the home today, but your father and I weren't sure you'd feel up to going." Her face still looked anxious.

"Oh, I do, Mom, absolutely."

"She looks fine, Rachel," said Sarah's father. "I think the visit will do us all good."

"I'm hungry, too," Sarah added. "That oatmeal for breakfast was gross."

"Well, I'm not sure how good the food will be, but Grandma Ruth really wants us to visit," her mother told her.

"I wonder if she remembers playing *dreidel* over the store," Sarah said to herself.

She didn't realize she had spoken aloud until her father said, "What's that? *Dreidel?*"

"Oh, nothing. I just wondered if they had *dreidels* back then, when she was a little girl and her family used the menorah." That wasn't really a lie, just not telling the whole truth.

Lunch at Lakeview Manor was actually pretty good: hot turkey sandwiches with a choice of salads and yummy desserts. Sarah had a slice of mince pie and some chocolate cake. "You must be feeling better — there's nothing wrong with your appetite today," her father joked. Even tiny Great-Grandma Ruth ate a generous piece of apple pie.

Ruth had dressed up for the occasion, wearing a purple sweater embroidered with flowers and a pair of grey pants. "I don't like staying in my housecoat all day, like some of them do," she said. Her eyes were bright behind her glasses, and her short, very white hair was brushed so it curled softly around her face. She even wore a touch of pink lipstick.

"What happened to you?" she asked when they first arrived, looking at the bandage, and Sarah told her she'd crashed her toboggan at Christie Pits.

"Do you play over there now?" Ruth asked. "I can never think of that place without remembering the fighting in ... 1935, was it? 1933? When Beatrice was a little girl. I had some friends who were hurt there. It was a bad time."

Sarah pricked up her ears, hoping to learn more — she was disappointed when her father changed the subject. "It was," he said, "and I know you can tell us a lot about it, but today let's think about happier things." I guess those memories will have to wait for another visit, thought Sarah.

"My mother was a wonderful baker," Ruth told them as she finished her pie. "She even invented an apple pastry. She was trying to make strudel but didn't have the patience to pull the dough really thin, like this" — she gestured with her hands — "so she rolled it out instead with a rolling pin. I got to help her sometimes. She'd put slices of apple mixed with raisins between the layers of pastry. If I was good, she'd give me a piece of raw apple dipped in sugar and cinnamon."

"I remember you used to make that, too," said Sarah's mother with a big smile. "It was my favourite dessert! And you would give me those pieces of apple."

"Yes, but my pastry wasn't as good as hers," said Ruth. "I remember like it was yesterday. Rolling the dough on our old kitchen table in the apartment above the store."

"She made *rugelah* too, didn't she?" Sarah asked.

Great-Grandma Ruth nodded. "Yes, yes, she did. With

apricot jam and nuts, when we could afford them. Usually around Hanukkah. She gave them away to visitors, even to customers at the store." She closed her eyes for a long moment.

"You're remembering a lot today, Bubie," said Sarah's mom.

Bubie — Sarah hadn't heard her mother call her grandmother that for a long time.

"Yes, yes, I am," Ruth nodded.

Just then one of the staff members led a group of residents toward the front of the dining room to sing carols while she played the piano. Sarah and her parents listened as the elderly voices gradually grew stronger and clearer. The group was happy; no one cared about missed words and flat notes. Sarah and her mother joined in when they sang "Jingle Bells" and "Frosty the Snowman." Her father didn't sing but he put his arm around Sarah's shoulder; she looked up and saw that he was smiling. Sarah noticed that some of the residents dozed in their chairs or wheelchairs during the singing, but she figured they heard the music anyway. There was one old woman, huddled under a pink and green afghan, who mouthed the words to all the songs even though she looked half-asleep. And a man wearing a bright red scarf waved his hands rhythmically, conducting music in the air.

Ruth hummed along to most of the songs. Finally, when there was a lull in the music, she got up carefully and used her walker to make her way to the piano. Sarah and her parents followed close behind. "I'd like to try," Ruth said timidly. "I used to play …"

"Of course, Mrs. Jacobs," said the worker, who wore a name tag that said "Stephanie" pinned to her shirt with a brooch shaped like sprig of holly.

Ruth sat down and began to pick out some notes, at first awkwardly, with trembling fingers, and then with more confidence. Even on the badly tuned old piano, the notes sounded pure and true.

"Chopin," breathed Sarah's mother. "A *Nocturne*. I didn't know she could still play like that."

The melody changed to part of the Mozart piece her mother had played a few nights earlier. The chatter in the room died down. Finally, Ruth drifted into a lilting tune that Sarah immediately recognized. As she played, Ruth sang Yiddish words in a soft, sweet voice. *"Rozhinkes mit mandlen, Dos vet zayn dayn baruf …*

"An old lullaby," Ruth said when she finished. "My mother, may her memory be a blessing, used to sing it to us, and my father played it on his …" She mimed playing a harmonica.

"Harmonica," Sarah said softly, and Ruth nodded.

"*Harmonike* in Yiddish. Almost the same word but I forgot it anyway. My father could make it sing like an angel."

No wonder the song was familiar. It was the lullaby Wolf had played on his harmonica, when they were on the ship, and the one Anna had sung to baby Ruth in the cemetery. "It's beautiful," Sarah whispered. Ruth's singing reminded her of the rich taste of raisins and almonds.

"So," said Ruth, "Enough noise from an old lady." She eased herself up from the piano bench and went to sit in an armchair nearby.

"I want to thank you, Great-Grandma — Bubie — for giving us your menorah," Sarah said, taking Ruth's thin hand in her own, then giving her a gentle hug. She smelled different today, fresh, like lemon soap. "It really meant a lot to me," she added.

"To all of us," said her mother.

"That is a special menorah," said Ruth. "I always liked watching the candles. Sometimes I thought I could see pictures in their flames. My mother told us that her grandmother said we should always take care of it and we would *zayn mit glik* — go with good luck."

Wow! Sarah thought. Ruth had seen things too — and even Anna's grandmother had known the menorah was special. Maybe it had always had the power to help people see what they needed to see.

"I walked through Kensington Market the other day," Sarah said. "It's so different now but I could picture you and your family in your store, long ago."

She wasn't sure her great-grandmother had heard her. But then Ruth said, "You're a good girl, Sarah. A *zisseh-maydela*, a sweet girl, sweet like sugar. I wish you could have seen me and my family in the old days. We had some good times. And you remind me of my big sister. You were named for her, you know."

"I wish I could have met her," Sarah said.

"But then you couldn't have been named Sarah," her

mother pointed out. "You know, I never met her either. She drove an ambulance in France during World War II and was killed by gunfire."

Ruth's eyes filled with tears. "Poor Sarah," she said. "She was so bossy, and so brave — she talked her way into going over there even when they said she was too old. Maybe better she shouldn't have gone."

Sarah turned away for a moment. Her lunch felt like a stone in her stomach. *Her* Sarah, who felt almost like a sister — killed in the war. So that's what her mother had meant by "dying young."

"You had another sister, too, didn't you?" asked Sarah's father.

"Miriam," said Ruth. "We called her Mimi. She went to New York and then Hollywood to be a writer. We lost touch but I know she worked on some movies out there. You met her once or twice, Rachel, in the early days when she still came to visit."

"I remember," said Sarah's mother. "She always wore lots of makeup and jewellery, and she let me spray on her perfume."

"Her daughter telephoned me when she died," said Ruth. "They had a very quiet funeral out there in California, but I was sick so I couldn't go. I was still in my apartment then, remember, Rachel? Poor Mimi."

So Mimi really did become a writer. Sarah wondered what films Mimi had worked on. Was there any way of finding out? She realized that Ruth had not mentioned David, the brother she had never known. Sarah wanted to ask about him, but a voice inside told her this wasn't the time.

The crowd in the room was thinning out and Ruth said she was tired, so they went back to her small, neat bedroom. When Ruth got into bed for a nap, Sarah thought she looked fragile, like a porcelain doll under the pink flowered quilt. Just as they were getting ready to leave, Ruth went into a coughing fit and her breath came in gasps. Sarah's father took her pulse and gave her one of the pills in a bottle by her bedside while Sarah poured her a glass of water. In a few minutes, Ruth had recovered. "I'm fine now. What's all the fuss about?"

But Sarah couldn't help thinking that her great-grandmother was so old, she would probably die soon. The thought worried her, but after Ben and all her experiences seeing people from the past, she thought she'd be able to cope with Ruth's death.

But what about Grandma B and Grandpa A? And Mom and Dad? She couldn't think about those possibilities, so she took a deep breath, exhaled and gave her mother's hand a warm squeeze. When they left, she kissed Ruth on the cheek. Her skin felt delicate as a flower petal.

After they got home, Sarah decided to ask her mother one more thing. She took the calendar off the kitchen wall and flipped to the picture of the butterfly from Terezin.

"Mom," she began, "did we have any relatives in the concentration camps?"

"Whatever makes you ask that, Sarah?"

"Well, this butterfly on the calendar is from a camp called

Terezin, and Marnie and I were talking about Anne Frank the other day, and … I was just wondering."

"That was a terrible time. The Holocaust. Maybe it seems long ago to you and your friends, but it's still very recent, and something no one should forget. And yes, I can tell you some things about our family. Come, sit down here on the couch," she said, putting her arm around Sarah.

"This is something Grandma B remembers from the time she was a little girl, younger than you are. Of course, her family had come to Canada years before, but she had cousins who lived in Prague, the capital of Czechoslovakia — what's now called the Czech Republic," she explained. "They were her father's cousins, and he and her mother — your great-grandmother Ruth — tried hard to get them to come to Canada, to be safe. But there were problems and delays, and eventually it was too late for them to escape. No one knew what happened to them until after the war, when they got a letter from one of the cousins, Pavel. He was the only one to survive. He went to Israel, and I think some of his children still live there."

Sarah's mother looked thoughtful. "You're getting older now, Sarah, and I'm glad you're asking about all this. Maybe we can take a trip to Israel sometime and try to look up Pavel's family." She sighed. "It was a terrible time. There were so many lost in the war, people we'll never know about."

Sarah felt a rush of sadness. She had never met Eva but she felt as though she knew her after watching Grandma B with the butterfly picture. At least she knew Eva's name. Another ghost, another person she wished she could have known.

"I believe Pavel and his sister Eva were at Terezin for a while," Sarah's mother was saying. "My mother and grandmother talked about them a lot, and for years we lit a candle for Eva and the rest of the family at Yom Kippur, to remember them. My mother had a picture that Eva drew and sent her before the war — it was a butterfly, too. The children did lots of drawings at Terezin, and it's a miracle that so many of those drawings survived when the children didn't." She looked more closely at the picture and the poem on the calendar. "It says 'Artist unknown.' You know, this looks just like Eva's butterfly. I wonder if …"

She wiped her eyes and turned to Sarah. "I think your grandmother still has the picture Eva sent her. You can ask her about it sometime. She keeps it in her jewellery box and she used to show it to me when I was little."

"I'd really like to see it," said Sarah. She remembered rummaging through Grandma B's leather jewellery box when she was younger; maybe she'd actually seen that picture and forgotten about it. Would it look like the picture she'd seen Bea admire through the magic of the menorah? She knew that someday she would tell her mother more about everything that had happened when she lit the candles.

"You know, Grandma B didn't mean to upset you when she gave you that locket the other night," Sarah's mother said gently. "I think — I think she was trying to say something without words. She's always been someone who loves mementoes, pictures, little keepsakes. I guess holding on to things helps her feel better. I don't think she realized how hard it would be for you. Clothes, pictures, even that old teddy bear … they make your dad and me sad, too, but they help us remember, and I guess that's good."

Then her father came in with steaming mugs of hot chocolate and they all sat together sipping the warm drinks. When they finished, Sarah said, "I think I'll just go up to my room and chill for a little while." She was feeling a bit tired. Her father walked upstairs with her, carrying her backpack.

"Sure your head is okay?" he asked.

"Sure, Dad," she said. "Ready to race again tomorrow."

"It's hard being a doctor and a parent, too, especially when it's your own kids who are sick," he told her. "You're still my favourite daughter, you know."

They exchanged a quick hug, then he went back downstairs. Sarah was alone.

She wanted to call Marnie and Raphael or send them an e-mail to let them know she was all right. But first she unpacked her things. She took the menorah out of the backpack and set it on the top shelf of her bookcase. It gleamed in the golden light of the late-afternoon sun, even without candles. Dribbles of coloured wax made random patterns on the brass. She propped Zachary up on her pillow so he could see it. Sarah didn't have to hide the bear now. She knew that her mother — and even her father — would understand. She took the crumpled square of Ben's blanket out of her dresser drawer and gave it to Zachary to hold. On impulse, she fastened the locket around the bear's furry neck, and gently touched the engraved rose.

She would have loved to tell Ben the story of the menorah

and how she had met all the relatives from the past. They were *his* relatives, too. But that couldn't happen, except in her mind. Still, if she wrote it down now so she didn't forget the details, she could tell the story to her own kids someday, the way she would have told it to Ben.

And anyway, maybe the story wasn't over. What would happen when she lit the candles next year?

NOTES

The lullaby "Raisins and Almonds" (First Day, Sixth Day and Ninth Day) is adapted from a Yiddish folk song, "Unter Yankeles Vigele," by Abraham Goldfadden for his operetta *Shulamis* (1880). There are several versions of the song, with different verses. The translations and variations in this book are by the author, Ellen S. Jaffe. Ruth Slater, former Cantor at Temple Anshe Sholom in Hamilton, provided the Yiddish text and one translation.

The lullaby, "May Your Heart Be Clear" — "*Zolstu zayn clor*" (Sixth Day) is from an original song by Honey Novick, c. 2005.

The description of the butterfly pictures and the words from the poem on Sarah's calendar are taken from drawings and a poem in the book *I Never Saw Another Butterfly: Children's Drawings and Poems from Terezin Concentration Camp, 1942-1944*, ed. Hana Volavkova, (New York: Schocken Books, 1978). Library of Congress number 64-15573, 67570. The poem on the picture sent to Beatrice by her cousins is the author's own creation. Many artists, writers and musicians were imprisoned in Terezin (Terezin in Czech, Theresienstadt in German) and they gave lessons to the children who were also prisoners there. Most of the inmates of Terezin later died at Auschwitz, though a few survived. Many of the childrens' poems and drawings, as well as artwork and pieces of music by adults, were preserved and brought to light after the war. Some of the butterfly pictures in the book are by Eva Bulova. Here is the full version of the published poem "The Butterfly," by Pavel Friedmann:

The last, the very last,
So richly, brightly, dazzlingly yellow
Perhaps if the sun's tears would sing
against a white stone ...
Such, such a yellow
Is carried lightly 'way up high
It went away I'm sure because it wished to
kiss the world goodbye.

For seven weeks I've lived in here,
Penned up inside this ghetto
        But I have found my people here,
        The dandelions call to me
And the white chestnut candles in the court.
Only, I never saw another butterfly.
That butterfly was the last one.
Butterflies don't live in here,
In the ghetto.

Sarah's book report is on the novel *False Face*, by Welwyn Wilton Katz (Toronto: Groundwood, 1987.)

Marnie's book report is on *Anne Frank: The Diary of a Young Girl*, which has been published in various editions and made into a play and a film.

The book *The Snow Cat* (Eighth Day) is by Dayal Kaur Khalsa, (Montreal: Tundra Books, 1992.)

Glossary*

Bar Mitzvah – the ceremony when a young person becomes a full member of the Jewish community. Boys have a Bar Mitzvah at age 13; girls have a Bat Mitzvah at age 12 or 13. The word "mitzvah"(plural "mitzvoth") means a religious commandment and also a good deed, an act of human kindness.

Bubie – grandmother

challah – delicious egg bread baked especially for Shabbat (pronounced "hallah")

dreidel – the four-sided spinning top which people use during Hanukkah, usually to play a children's "gambling" game with raisins, almonds, pennies, etc.

feh – an expression of displeasure, disapproval, disgust

gelt – money. Chocolate coins wrapped in gold foil, given as a treat or for playing the dreidel game, are referred to as Hanukkah *gelt*.

glik – luck

harmonike – harmonica

Keneinahora – words to keep away the evil eye, usually said when you are talking about something good happening, so you don't seem too proud or sure of yourself.

Kislev – a month of the Jewish calendar, occurring in November/December. Hanukkah always begins on the eve of the 25th day of Kislev. (Jewish days are counted from sundown to sundown.)

Kristallnacht – literally, "Crystal Night," or "the Night of

Broken Glass." The name given to the nights of November 9 and 10, 1938, in Germany, Austria and the Sudetenland (part of Czechoslovakia), countries which the German (Nazi) government took over in 1938. This was a massive, government-initiated attack by soldiers and mobs of people on Jewish businesses, synagogues, cemeteries, schools and homes. Not only were windows smashed, but over 1000 synagogues were burnt, 7500 businesses destroyed, about 100 people killed and many more wounded, and 30,000 people were arrested and sent to concentration camps. Kristallnacht marked a turning point in the escalation of terror leading to World War II and the Holocaust.

latkes – potato pancakes, usually eaten at Hanukkah, often served with applesauce and sour cream

mandelbrot – an almond cookie, hard and rectangular like a biscotti. (Also the last name of a famous mathematician, Benoit Mandelbrot.)

menorah – a nine-branched candle-holder used at Hanukkah; the place for the ninth candle, the *Shamas* (see below) is set apart from the rest. There are many styles of menorah, both ancient and modern: fancy or plain, made of metal, pottery, glass, etc. Another name for this candle-holder is *hanukiah*, and *menorah* can also refer to the seven-branched candle-holder that is another symbol of Judaism.

maydela – a young girl

meyn kind/meyn kinder – my child/my children

mitgefil – condolences (as after a death)

nun, gimel, hay, shin – Hebrew letters, each printed on one of the four faces of the dreidel. They give instructions for playing the game and also are the initials of the words *Nes gadol haya sham*, "A great miracle happened there," referring to Hanukkah.

rugelah – small cakes made of rolled triangles of dough, filled with raisins, almonds, jam, etc. and then baked (if you're very lucky, you'll find ones with chocolate filling!)

sha – "Shhh," a comfort word used with babies, small children and others who need soothing.

Shamas – the "helper" candle, used to light the other Hanukkah candles on the menorah; derived from a word that means "servant."

sheitel – the wig worn by Orthodox Jewish women after they marry and cut their hair short.

Shiveh (or *Shiva*) – the seven days of mourning after the funeral of a loved one. Observing this mourning is called "sitting Shiveh." Prayers are said and visitors call on the family; some people may observe customs such as covering all the mirrors in the house during this time. The word shiveh literally means "seven."

(Shiva, mentioned in the story as the name of a shop in the modern Kensington Market, is also the Hindu god of creation and destruction).

shtetl – small Eastern European villages populated by Jews, a term used mainly for communities in the 19th century.

shul – a familiar word for synagogue

Tante – aunt. The same word is used for "aunt" in German, Yiddish and French.

Tateleh – "little man," a term of endearment and affection for a baby boy or young son.

Torah – the Five Books of Moses, or the first five books of the Bible. The Torah is inscribed on a scroll of parchment which is kept in a special place in the synagogue, called the Ark. Each week, a passage is read aloud on the Sabbath, and the scroll is carried through the synagogue so people can see and touch it. The Torah tells the story of the beginning of the Jewish people, and contains the laws they should live by.

tsouris – trouble, things that make you upset

yarmulke – the skullcap worn in the synagogue by Jewish men (and some women, in Reform synagogues), and at all times by men who are devout

zayn mit glik – go with luck

zisseh – sweet; *zisseh-maydela* is a sweet little girl

* Many Yiddish words have various spellings in English. We have tried to select the most accepted and commonly used ones.

Acknowledgements

In addition to the people named in the dedication, many people contributed to this book.

I thank all the editors at Sumach Press for believing in this story, especially Jennifer Day for bringing it to fruition. This is my second opportunity to work with Sumach, and I appreciate their professional yet friendly attitude, their respect for authors and illustrators and their attention to detail. Jennifer's patience, persistence and perceptiveness were especially helpful.

I also owe particular and deep thanks to Catherine Marjoribanks for her sensitive, skillful reading and editing which helped the book find its shape and voice. I also enjoyed her calm cheerfulness when I fell prone to "author's angst."

I am grateful to the Ontario Arts Council for giving me a Writers' Reserve Grant to help complete this book, allowing both writing time and travel time.

Many people helped with specific information and insight. Thanks (in no definite order) to: Al Berns and Ruby Berns for telling me about life in the Kensington Market area and on Crawford Street at the time of the Christie Pits riots; Ruth Slater for giving me the text of the lullaby "Raisins and Almonds" and for her beautiful singing of Yiddish lullabies and songs as well as Jewish cantorial music; Honey Novick for creating the lullaby *"Zolstu zayn clor"* ("May Your Heart Be Clear") especially for this story; Talia Kollek for reading the book with a 13-year-old's eye, and to other young readers of earlier versions (Debbie and Karen Kohn, Monica and Gillian Black); Gilda Mekler for her suggestions regarding the "Seventh Day" chapter, the owner of the "Eye of Shiva" shop on Kensington Street, Toronto, for her reminiscences of visits to Kensington Market as a child; Laura Wolfson and Phyllis Knight and her son Asher Knight for their information about matters relating to Judaism; Charly Chiarelli for making Wolf's harmonica come alive and "sing"; Dr. Ellen B. Ryan, with whom I worked on the subject of stories and memory; John (Yonah) Yaphe for medical consultation; Barry Bender for help with translations and other information; and both Barry Bender and Norma Jack for making me welcome in their home on ordinary days as well as holiday celebrations; J.J. Steinfeld for his advice to my muse.

Thanks to the congregation of Temple Anshe Sholom and to the residents and staff of Shalom Village Apartments and Nursing Home in Hamilton, Ontario.

Two educational programs in which I work have given a meaningful context to the book:

Working Family Treasures, sponsored by the Ontario Workers Arts and Heritage Centre in Hamilton, has shown that many young people are interested in discovering their family treasures and family stories, and that older people enjoy sharing these stories. *Learning Through the Arts*™, operated through the Royal Conservatory of Music in Toronto, demonstrates the importance of the arts in all aspects of learning, for students and teachers of all ages.

All the people I have worked with in writing groups over the years have helped me shape my style, sharpen my focus and deepen my understanding of writing from the heart as well as the mind. My friends and colleagues have been patient and encouraging during the writing process.

Special thanks to Chris Lounsberry of Systems Support for his technical support and advice.

And thanks to the owners and staff of the Algonquin Lake Inn, where I spent some time working on this book — with the added pleasure (which Raphael would have shared) of seeing two moose and a wolf in Algonquin Park.

This book is about family, and I would like to give lasting and deep thanks to my mother Viola (Albert) Jaffe and my son Joe Albert Bitz for their steadfast love and support, and to the beloved memory of many other members of my family, including Rose (Axelrod) Albert and Lou Albert, Zelda Axelrod, Sarah Jaffe and Samuel Jaffe, Betty (Jaffe) Marshall and Fay (Jaffe) Gruber and my father, Harry L. Jaffe.

Finally, people ask how writers get their ideas. A better question is "how do the ideas get you?" I have been living with Sarah and her family and friends for a long time, getting to know more about their lives. I want to thank my lovely characters and I hope they have not been disappointed in their search for an author to tell their story.

Other Books for Young Adults from Sumach Press

Find out more at www.sumachpress.com